ABOUT THIS BOOK

What do you do when Death is in love with you?

Monte Tayute, laid-back biker and skilled computer hacker, has been haunted by visions of a gorgeous woman in black. It's an endless dream with the two meeting on a dark road at Samhain. Nothing the nagual shifter tries seems to rid him of the constant image now playing havoc with his life.

In a different realm, Pandora is having her own recurring vision. Hers is of a man who rides a motorcycle on a lonely road. The shinigami—a death spirit of the Japanese underworld—doesn't want hers to stop. On the contrary, Pandora wants to know if the man is real.

When life meets death, the sparks fly. Monte allows Pandora to experience pleasure and love for the first time. Unfortunately, there's an entity who's been waiting on Pandora for over a century, and he's not playing around.

Pandora is supposed to become Death's bride, but Monte isn't ready to give her up.

It all comes down to a game between the shifter and Death. If Monte plays the cards right, he might cheat Death and keep Pandora. Fail, and Death will be the only one happy.

HAVENWOOD FALLS
SIN & SILK BOOKS

Taming the Beast by Nadirah Foxx

Plans Laid Bare by J.D. Nelson

Shift of Fate by Victoria Escobar

Stolen Wishes by Victoria Flynn

Damned Allure by Justine Winter

Savage Salvation by Kristie Cook

Dark Seduction by Michele G. Miller & R.K. Ryals

Soul Laid Bare by J.D. Nelson

Stray With Me by E.J. Fechenda

Chase the Flames by Desiree Lafawn

Flirting With Death by Nadirah Foxx

Also try the signature line, Havenwood Falls, the historical paranormal line, Legends of Havenwood Falls, and stories from the local supernatural college in Sun & Moon Academy.

Stay up to date at www.HavenwoodFalls.com

BOOKS BY NADIRAH FOXX

FLIRTING WITH DEATH

NADIRAH FOXX

Be careful what you hope for.

CHAPTER 1

PANDORA

The soft din of humans chattering was a pleasant change from the usual nothingness. I glanced around the dimly lit sushi restaurant, admiring the different colors and expression-filled faces. It was all so different from Yomi-no-kuni—the Japanese shadow realm. The murky netherworld only contained shades of gray.

"What can I get you?" asked a bartender.

I smiled. "Moscato."

My mark was late, but I was good with that. It gave me more time to appreciate earthly things. The server brought my white wine, and I reached for my purse.

"Allow me." The deep voice was unfamiliar.

Hoping it might be my target, I looked up and gasped. The man beside me was larger than life, with hair darker than a raven's feathers and eyes like obsidian. He wore a tailored onyx-colored suit and a matching shirt and tie. If it hadn't been for his wide, too-bright grin, it would have been like staring into darkness. Despite the gloomy exterior, the man was handsome.

He leaned in. "Forgive my interruption. I noticed you were alone."

I batted my eyelashes like an idiot. "Not for long." Before he got the wrong idea, I added, "I'm meeting someone."

His eyebrows arched. "Then I should leave. I wouldn't want your date to jump to any conclusions."

"Not a date. It's a . . ."

I nearly slipped up and told the gorgeous stranger that I was an escort. It was something my kind didn't reveal because of the issues humans had with the concept. They believed that *all* companions were in the business of sex for hire. Well . . . I did get paid and sex sometimes happened, but it wasn't my purpose. I was a shinigami escort—a death spirit who guided souls to the afterlife.

"A what?" the man asked politely.

"It's a business meeting," I replied.

The stranger nodded. "Understood. Perhaps when you're done, we could get to know each other?"

If I were allowed the luxury of a private life, I would entertain the thought. Instead, I opened my bag and removed my business card. I fingered the red embossed torii—a Japanese gate—with my name beneath it. If the man phoned, he'd receive a recorded message saying the number was out of service. I hated the deception, but it wasn't as if I'd see him again. He wasn't the type to be on my list.

"Give me a call." I handed him the white card.

"I'll do that." He pocketed the item, smiled, and said, "You have a great evening, Pandora."

I watched him walk to the exit and then noticed my date. Sadly, it wouldn't be a wonderful night. A bright ethereal glow surrounded the overweight salesman. He was only hours away from death claiming him. This job should be an easy one.

The previous night's target was exhausting. Instead of the traveling salesman giving over to death, he lingered as his soul tried desperately to stay on earth.

His dark eye sockets widen as his diaphanous body shimmers. "Why? I have a wife . . . children . . . They need me."

"Not anymore. It is your time." I wrap my hand around his wrist.

"No!"

I hate stubborn souls. My goal is to entice someone to the afterlife, not drag them. Sometimes, however, I have to resort to darker measures. The flesh suit I regularly wear disintegrates, leaving behind my true skeletal form. My face elongates and sharp, pointed teeth appear as my bluish lips part. I wail like a banshee.

The ear-piercing screech nearly unravels the businessman's spirit as he scurries toward the bright light. When the portal closes, my job is done, and I slink away, reconstructing my corporeal form as I go.

I was made for pleasure, but when needed to, I could scare the shit out of anyone.

Gazing out my apartment window, I tried to put the episode out of my mind, but the colorless realm didn't help. There was nothing in Yomi-no-kuni to please the eye. No division between sky and land. No green grass or flowers to gaze upon. Only shadows and endless phantasms—other death spirits and souls punished for all eternity.

I was frustrated, and the reluctant salesman didn't help. It was supposed to be a two-night engagement—one to get to know him, and the second to escort him into the great beyond. It didn't happen that way. Instead, I only had the one night with him, but Madame Izanami—a.k.a. Madame Death—didn't care as long as the job was done.

In all honesty, shinigami had a better existence than what normal reapers endured. Death's creations didn't hang around anywhere for long or maintain corporeal forms. shinigami did both.

Some called us monsters or creatures of darkness. Not entirely false, but without shinigami, souls would flounder and exist as ghosts. With us, they got a choice—a ghostly existence or a glorious afterlife. Most chose the latter.

Thankfully, the disparaging names didn't bother me. As I drew out a man's last breath, I heard more scintillating ones. Honestly, was it wrong for humans to die with a smile on their faces? I wasn't ashamed of what I did, but lately I'd wanted something else.

Something more than taking all the time. Death spirits were hard-wired for harvesting. Most of us had no issue with it, but I wasn't like everyone else. I wanted to see what it was like to receive—passion, love, even friendship.

Don't get it twisted. I wasn't some flighty female dying to hop into bed with each and every mark on my list. The night didn't always end up between the sheets. Some men liked talking and having their ego stroked. It was an admirable way of counting down to the end of a life. But then there were the ones who preferred having their dicks stroked instead. Hey, whatever floated their boats—I didn't judge. It got the job done, but it wasn't enough for me anymore.

In two hundred years, I had yet to experience my own gratification. Talk about major dissatisfaction. Not one man aroused me, taking me to the edge of passion and back again.

When I complained, I received reminders that delight was not something afforded to our kind. In a nutshell, we didn't get to love. The emotion supposedly clouded our judgment and kept us from doing our job. I didn't care. I wanted my chance. Just one night of undying (pun intended) passion in a man's arms.

My bellyaching got so bad that the other death spirits filed grievances, and Madame Death had called me to her cold, dark corner office.

Madame's assistant, a handsome shinigami named Toshi, rakes his black eyes over me and offers a toothy smile. "When you're done with her, how about you and me go out tonight?"

"Not in a million years," I say, and push open the door.

A blast of frigid air hits me, and my form flickers, losing its cohesiveness. The mist, full of despair, parts, and the figure of a woman emerges. Madame is more of a shade than the embodiment of an entity. The gossips claim that the goddess is only a corpse with rotting flesh and maggots crawling in and out of her orifices. Not something I want to view, whether it's true or not.

"Takara, do you know why you're here?"

Madame only uses my given name when I'm in trouble. Realizing the seriousness of the summons, I keep quiet.

"Sit down," she orders.

After I'm seated, she continues, "I'm giving you a chance to explain yourself. I've listened to numerous allegations, and I'm not pleased. Why the constant complaints? This sort of thing isn't like you."

Averting my eyes, I say, "Ma'am, I'm sorry. It's nothing. I just had a bad night."

Although I can't see her stare, I feel its frostiness. She exhales. "Takara, you are one of my best creations. It pains me to see you so disillusioned. Our lot in this world is to guide souls to their final resting place. Love isn't in the equation."

"I know," I say meekly.

"Do you?" Her fingers tap an unseen surface—the only noise in the

void—as if my employer is considering her words. "It sets a bad precedent when those at the top of the heap start whining. Continue to do so, and I'll be forced to take you off active duty."

My gaze whips up. "A desk job would kill me."

"A bit of an exaggeration, don't you think? I'd rather confine you than have you bring down morale."

A suspension is much better than the alternative—the worst fate for shinigami. With one snap of Madame's fingers, I could become one of the shadows attached to Yomi-no-kuni.

"Then stop the griping, Takara. We have one job, and one job only. Personal satisfaction comes with successfully completing a task."

"Understood," I say with more conviction than I feel.

"I hope so. I'd rather give out rewards than punishments any day."

That was a week ago. Since then I'd been on my best behavior. I kept my thoughts focused, and when I got bored, I took on extra assignments. It worked for seven agonizingly long days and then it stopped.

My Rattler social media feed pinged on my phone. I turned my attention to the flat-screen television on the wall. DNN—the Death News Network—displayed yet another fatal car crash. The channel was how death spirits got the news of human expirations. Unfortunately, DNN and Rattler were permanent fixtures. You couldn't turn them off, but I could mute the TV. My black stilettos clicked across the floor as I headed to the coffee table in search of the remote.

Before I reached it, the doorbell rang. Odd. I wasn't expecting anyone, and my roommate was out for the evening.

I glanced at my appearance in the full-length mirror. Fortunately, head-to-toe black leather was enjoyed by a lot of the humans I was set up with. I fluffed my ebony-colored hair, applied another coat of Deadly Decay lipstick in Drop Dead Red, and drew in a breath before opening the door.

The handsome stranger from the restaurant was on the other side. How was that possible?

"May I come in, Takara?"

I was too stunned to refuse. *How did he know my given name?*

He was so tall that he had to duck to clear the doorway. Once inside, he went to the sofa and made himself comfortable as if it were a normal thing for him to visit me.

Standing with my hand on the knob, I asked, "How are you here? *What* are you?"

"Death, of course." He spread his long arms over the back of my sofa and crossed his ankle over a knee. "I thought it time we officially met."

Normally, death spirits could sense other supernaturals. But forces, like Death, had a way of screwing with our radar so that we didn't discern them. But why was he there?

Still confused, I joined him in the living room but kept my distance. "And why is that?"

He sighed. "It's customary for a bride-to-be to meet her groom."

My mouth fell open.

Ignoring my silence, Death continued, "It's amazing how your mood has changed since our first meeting. Not important, though. I thought we'd start with dinner on Samhain. We can dine here, or I can take you someplace special."

Dinner with Death?

Was he fucking kidding me?

It was true that I wanted something more, but not with a chaotic entity.

"Takara, is there something wrong?" His dark, lust-filled gaze raked over me, and suddenly I felt naked. "Come sit down. I'd like to get to know you better."

He needed to stop saying that. It wasn't happening.

Thankfully, the door opened behind me. Turning around, I saw Hope—my roommate and created twin. Madame gave us the same waist-length black wavy hair, too-pale skin, and curvy figure. Shinigami are supposed to work in pairs, and she was my designated partner. Sometimes, like the night with the salesman, we got to work alone.

The only obvious difference between Hope and me were our almond-shaped eyes. Mine were deep green while hers were cerulean blue, earning us our listing in the home office's database as Emerald and Sapphire. In the human world, we had supernatural contacts who trolled the various dating services searching for possible marks. If someone said they were into twins or loved green or blue eyes, we were messaged.

"Who's this?" she asked.

"Hope, meet Death."

Her jaw dropped, mimicking my earlier expression.

He pushed to his large feet and walked toward us. "It's a pleasure to meet you, Hope." He placed his enormous hand on my shoulder. "I'll leave now, but will expect you for dinner on Samhain."

I shook my head. "I'm sorry, but I'll have to decline."

Death squeezed, and pain shot through my body, threatening to unravel my corporeal form. "Not an option. Nobody turns me down."

I swallowed hard. Hope's worried gaze landed on me.

He eased up his grip and dropped his hand. "Something you should know about me, Takara. When I want something—or someone—I get it. You were promised to me. You shall fulfill your obligation. Don't cross me. I assure you that my punishment would be worse than anything Izanami could do to you."

He stalked toward the door.

After it closed, Hope asked, "What the fuck was that about? What did he mean by you're promised to him?"

"I don't know, but I don't plan on sticking around to find out." Reluctantly, I told her what Death told me.

"If you're supposed to marry an entity—"

"I won't do it. There are other things I want to do."

The man I had been dreaming of for years came to mind. He was tall, mysterious, and rode a motorcycle. If I was about to be shackled for all eternity to Death, maybe it was time to see if the man was real.

CHAPTER 2

MONTE

I placed a few bills on the counter and waved goodnight to Liam and the brothers. Most likely, they'd hang out at the Dirty Knuckle for another hour or so, tossing back drinks and catching up. The MC had been busy all week making runs for Cerberus Delivery. I was worn out and ready for a little relaxation.

Hunter looked up from his bottle of beer. "Heading out so soon?"

"Yeah. I'm beat."

My best friend's jaw dropped. "You okay? Not going up into the mountains and stretching your legs?"

That was me—the guy with habits so predictable that everybody knew my patterns. "Not tonight. Join me in the morning?"

Hunter's lips curled up on one side. "Naw. It'll take more than a chance to run free to get me away from Izzie's side that early."

I chuckled. We didn't hang out much since he got hitched. Honestly, it didn't bother me. Just a hiccup in my usual routine.

One of the new prospects—a young vampire who could easily pose for Vampires Quarterly—had the nerve to joke about my cutting out early. I ignored the kid. The last time I hung out with the MC at a bar, I left with an attractive babe only to wake up the next day with a handcuff on one wrist. I had to endure a few hours of ribbing from the fellas as I waited for someone to arrive with a key. Someone could have cut it off, but they had more fun watching me squirm.

As I stepped outside, the faint scent of burning hickory carried on the breeze, and I inhaled deeply. It was a crisp, clear autumn night in Havenwood Falls. The perfect weather for that run Hunter mentioned. My beast stirred under my skin, dying to break forth and enjoy the mountain air. He'd have to take a back seat, though. Hoping for a decent night's sleep, I cranked up my bike and headed for home.

Stretching out on my black leather sofa, I picked up the remote, thinking I'd watch a little TV before calling it a night. It was wishful thinking. Of late, sleep was unattainable, leaving me staring up at the ceiling for hours. When I couldn't take it anymore, I'd get up and do some much-needed work on the small Victorian house I purchased a year ago. It was taking me a while to get the overhaul done since I'd been dragging my feet, not wanting to face the major task.

It was a boring existence, but one that I chose. After living on the wild side as a kid, it was better to live on the dull side. Before my family relocated me to Havenwood Falls, I'd landed myself in trouble with the authorities. After moving, I promised my grandparents that I'd behave—I owed them that much. After all, I could be serving time in a penitentiary if it weren't for them.

The insomnia had become a serious problem, but it made no sense. I had no real issues other than a sense that something was missing in my life. Like I should have something more, but I couldn't put my finger on it.

The problem wasn't my job. I enjoyed tinkering with engines, and Joshua Breen—the human who owned Havenwood Falls Garage & Tow Service—was a decent person. He'd get no complaints from me as long as I could do what I love.

And if I wasn't at the shop with my head under a hood, I was at the clubhouse repairing bikes or searching the darknet. The issue sure as hell wasn't with SIN or its members. There wasn't a damned thing I wouldn't do for my brothers. But hanging out with a bunch of men only went so far. I longed for something—no, someone—who could do for me what they couldn't. Which brought me back to my recent struggle with catching some z's. It started a month ago with a recurring dream.

I'm on my bike riding home. For Samhain, the winding road is unusually quiet, but I'm completely content without a care on my mind. Suddenly, I hit a slick spot, and I'm spinning out of control. The world blurs as I come to a stop, but something's not right. I'm upside down, and everything is hazy. A sound—like bullets punching the asphalt—comes closer. Blinking a few times, I see a pair of black high heels. My gaze travels up a shapely, leather-clad leg.

A voice like that of an angel speaks directly to my mind. "It's not your time."

Every night it was the same damned dream. On occasion, the woman didn't arrive, and the landscape faded to black. I had no idea what it meant, but each time it jarred me awake and kept me from sleeping.

At one point, it got so bad that I went to see Teeny Weeny Tahini, the clairvoyant. She told me that it might not be a simple dream, but more like one of those vision quests Hunter's grandfather went on. Her suggestion? Try a special blend of tea before bed. If the sleeplessness got worse, she wanted me to talk to Mayor Barbie Stuart. The woman was human but had an uncanny ability to interpret dreams. I told Teeny I'd consider the tea.

Yeah, right.

Instead, I made a beeline to the Circle J dispensary and let Adrian Roca fix me up with a little herbal sleep aid. Combined with some hard work around the house and a hot shower, a joint smoothed out my thoughts and allowed a few hours of bliss.

But it didn't erase the loneliness.

Nothing did that.

Up until a week ago, I was floating by with my routine, and the dreams weren't as bad. Then they escalated and knocked me sideways. Honestly, I hadn't slept in a few nights. One joint threatened to become two. I had to do something fast before I ended up like Bent Brent.

∾

As I watched the sun rise from my vantage point on top of Mount Alexa, I decided to call the mayor. It was either that or pay a visit to Rose Howe and see if the witch could hook me up with a potion or something.

An hour later, my doorbell rang. On the other side of the door was a tall, intimidating woman with one of those 1950s hairdos—all poufy and stiff. She smiled and said, "Good morning, Monte. Have I caught you at a bad time?"

I was slightly puzzled. After all, I called her. Then I remembered I had on my jacket. "No, no. Come on in."

"Were you on your way out? I can come back."

"Force of habit, I'm afraid." I shut the door before removing the outer garment. "I'm usually on my way to work by now."

She nodded and sat on the sofa, wrinkling her nose. "Madame Tahini told me about your difficulty. Could you tell me the dream?"

I took a seat on the recliner and relayed the details of my lingering nightmare. When I finished, Mayor Stuart blinked her azure-blue eyes and drew in a deep breath.

"And?"

She exhaled and said, "Of course, the um . . . obvious interpretation is an accident. Maybe it's just a run-of-the-mill mishap on your bike. I wouldn't call it a brush with death."

A brush with death?

Her words reminded me of what my grandfather said when I first started riding. That was ten years ago, and I'd never had an accident. Maybe my luck was coming to an end.

Mayor Stuart cleared her throat and pushed to her feet. "Was there a date or maybe a specific time in the dream?"

"There were Halloween decorations."

"Well, maybe you saw it in one of those Halloween movies. What we watch on television can influence our dreams. Honestly, it might not be anything but a suggestion that your life might be changing. Either way, if it is more serious, maybe don't ride on Halloween night? Too many people on the road, anyway." She started for the door, stopped, and faced me. "Oh, and Monte?"

"Yeah?"

"You might find valerian a better choice as a sleep aid." When I gave her a blank stare, she added, "It's not as risky."

Awareness hit me. She smelled the weed. I chuckled nervously and thanked her as I walked her out.

Needless to say, without enough sleep I wasn't up to going into the shop. Thankfully, Joshua understood and gave me a few days off. I spent the morning putting down new sod in the front yard—autumn was the perfect time for the chore. By afternoon, I was ready for more coffee and a meal.

Halloween had to be the favorite holiday for the entire town. Every shop was decked out in all sorts of spooky decor, from thick cobwebs and skeletons in windows to orange and black lights strung up like Christmas bulbs. I made a mental note to pick up candy for the trick-or-treaters and then I saw Rose outside of Howe's Herbal Shoppe.

The ginger-haired beauty smiled as I approached. "Afternoon, Monte. Back for more tea?"

"Not sure. Mayor Stuart suggested I try some valerian to help me sleep."

Rose's brow wrinkled. "You sound skeptical."

"Nothing I've tried so far has helped."

She crooked her finger. "Follow me. I have something that might do the trick."

As I trailed behind her, I asked, "It's not going to require something magical to wake me back up, will it?"

She laughed. "Nothing that intense. It just has a little more oomph to guarantee a good night's rest. Is there something going on I should know about?"

I perused a shelf of elixirs and said over my shoulder, "Just my dreams getting the best of me."

"I can fix that," she offered.

"I'll just take that hyped-up tea." It paid to be mindful with witches. One never knew what actually went into their concoctions.

"Okay. I have to grab it from the back."

I brewed the smelly tea as directed, and then sat staring at the mug, unsure if I should digest the contents. Rose assured me that I had nothing to worry about. I had my doubts, but tossed back the drink. I turned off the light and lay down.

The last of the trick-or-treaters traipse down my porch steps. I close the door and collapse onto the sofa. Tonight, I'm going to catch up on Supernatural—*almost required viewing on Samhain.*

Sadly, restlessness won't leave me alone. I end up turning off the brothers right in the middle of their mission, grab my jacket and keys, and head for the door. I'm on my bike headed up Main Street when I get the idea to check in on Hunter and Izzie.

Instead of continuing straight, I take the turn onto Blackstone Road and then steer into Creekwood Estates. The road curves, and silence surrounds me. Odd for Samhain. I would have thought the streets would be busy with partygoers.

I'm at peace for a change. Totally rested. Not a care on my mind.

Suddenly, the front tire skids. I'm spinning out of control.

Shit.

The tire hits the curb, and I tumble over the handle bars. My back collides with the concrete, and the landscape blurs. I blink to clear my gaze, but my vision remains fuzzy. Then I hear the thud of heels on the asphalt. When they stop, someone in black high heels comes into view. Leather squeaks as she crouches beside me.

The stranger touches my temple. "Not tonight. Don't worry. It's not your time yet. Tomorrow . . ."

My eyes popped open. Despite the heavy blankets, I was shivering. Slowly, I sat up. My sheets were damp, and my body was covered in sweat. I reached for my phone. It was only two in the morning. I ran my hand across my face. If the dream was a premonition, then I was about to celebrate my last Samhain.

CHAPTER 3

MONTE

The dream freaked the fuck out of me. I couldn't go back to sleep and didn't want to be alone. I refused to call Hunter, though. The man was married and had every right to enjoy some quality time with his wife. As the sun began to rise, I summoned up the courage and got out of bed. If it was going to be my last day on earth, I wasn't spending it like a damned coward.

After a ridiculously long hot shower, I dressed and headed into the kitchen. There was a lot of work to do. So much had to be replaced—the floor, the cabinets, and the tile. I'd picked out some possible paint choices and had the swatches laid out on the counter. None of it seemed important anymore. Same thing with every room in the house. Nobody should spend their final hours contemplating what should have been done.

I grabbed my keys and stalked out of the room, determined to find some fun—or make some. I didn't want to die alone and miserable. Opening the front door, I was surprised to see Hunter.

"Hey, man," I said.

"Hey, yourself." He pushed past me. "Got a minute?"

"Minutes are precious, Hunter." I closed the door and leaned against it. "What's up?"

"Baba had a vision." A pained expression twisted my friend's face. "Sit down, Monte."

Ordinarily, his worried tone would have concerned me, but after

14

last night's dream, I had a feeling I knew its cause. I strolled over to the sofa and dropped beside Hunter. "He saw me?"

He swallowed hard. "Yeah." Hunter paused for a beat or two. "Stay the fuck off your bike for a while. At least until we find a way around—"

"Can't fucking cheat death. You know that." When your number's up, there was nothing that could be done. No matter how good you thought you were at escaping it, Death caught up and claimed what was his.

"No, I'm not . . ." Hunter's voice wavered. He cleared his throat and tried again. "I'm not accepting that. Neither are you."

I bobbed my head. Arguing with him was a waste of time. I wanted to go out surrounded by my brothers and my best friend, not sniveling like a damned idiot. I slapped his leg. "Let's get the fuck out of here. Head over to the clubhouse and have some fun."

Hunter fixed me with an incredulous stare. "What the fuck? Are you—"

"Dead—" Poor choice of words. "I'm serious. Did you drive over?"

"Yeah. Truck's out front," he said absently.

"Good. Call Izzie. Tell her we need food, and a few of those dancers from Silk. I'm ready for a damned party."

My friend struggled to smile. Instead he shook his head, pushed to his feet, and pulled out his phone. "I'm on it. Meet you outside."

"Give me a few minutes."

I watched Hunter leave and then closed my eyes. It was the day of Samhain. Despite knowing what was coming, I refused to let it shake me. If I didn't get out and do something, I was going to hole up in this house and wait for the end. I clumped to the door. Time to face the world one last time.

The fellas thought Hunter and I had lost our damned minds. Who had an impromptu party before noon? The SIN clubhouse was full of scantily clad women. A wide variety of food covered the tables—mostly breakfast dishes because hey, who served pizza for breakfast?

I was a little shocked to see Senora Graves, the empusa, in the crowd. The brown-skinned woman gave me a curious gaze before she jerked a thumb toward the hallway. I followed her shapely ass toward the offices. We ducked into the main one—used for meetings.

Senora closed the door behind her. "What's up with this shindig?"

I shrugged. "Just shaking things up."

She folded her arms. "Uh-uh. I didn't buy it when Izzie asked me to help her bring over the food. If I didn't know better, I'd say this was the last hurrah for a dying man."

I pulled out a chair and straddled it. "What if it was?"

Her dark eyes bulged. "You're serious? Are you sick? What's going on?"

"Nothing like that. Been having visions. Supposedly, I'm gonna hop on my bike tonight and have a fatal accident." Saying it out loud made it more real. Maybe I could convince Rose Howe to spell me so that I just slept my way into the next life.

Senora touched my hand. "I'm sorry. I guess it's true what humans say."

"About?"

"The good dying young."

"Gee, thanks." Honestly, I didn't expect sympathy—or anything else—from her.

I swore the empusa's cheeks darkened. "No, I didn't mean—"

"It's okay, Senora. I'm good. That's why the party. No sitting around feeling sorry for myself. Everyone doesn't get a long life."

No. I didn't believe that bullshit, but what else was I supposed to do? I was an adult, not a child. As much as I wanted to pitch a fit, scream until heaven and earth—and possibly hell too—all stood still, I wouldn't. It wasn't my style. People knew me as being laid-back to a fault. I wasn't about to disappoint.

I made sure my smile was locked in place as I stood. "Come on, Senora. Look, nobody else is questioning it. Just help me celebrate."

She looked at me with watery eyes. "I-I can't."

"You can. Hey . . ." If that was indeed my last day on earth, maybe I could put aside my concerns about fucking an empusa. "Why don't we—"

"Pass." She wiped away an errant tear. "I'm a fighter. If it were me, I'd retaliate. I'd tell Death to kiss my ass. You haven't done shit yet. No girlfriend. No family. Where's your legacy, Monte?"

"Doesn't matter," I lied.

"The fuck it doesn't!" She marched over to the door. "If you won't fight, don't ask me to stand by and watch. I thought you were stronger than that."

"Senora."

"Don't, Monte." She drew in a deep breath and in a calmer voice said, "Go talk to Baba about his vision. Maybe there's a message for you."

"What do you mean?" I thought it was crystal clear. I'm going to die. End of story—*my* story.

"What if the dying has to do with the life you're living? Instead of continuing on the same path, maybe a new one is about to start."

I tilted my head to one side. "Not a literal death then?"

"Exactly. Maybe you just need to be open to change. Consider it and stop acting like a fucking idiot." Senora slammed the door behind her.

Maybe there was some validity in Senora's words. I'd been thinking a lot about changing things in my life. Maybe the dream was a reflection of my thoughts. I left the office and slipped out the rear exit.

On foot, it took longer than usual to reach Creekwood Estates. It gave me plenty of time to think. For starters, I never thought Senora would have cared one way or another if I lived or died. Outside of my helping her out during that nonsense with the Collector, we didn't know each other. We weren't friends, but maybe that was what I needed—a stranger to slap some sense into me. Perhaps it was time to stop letting life pass me by.

Baba opened the door before I rang the bell. The old man didn't speak. He simply turned and shuffled down the hall. I followed him into the great room.

"Have a seat, Montezuma." Hunter's grandfather had a colorful rug spread in front of the fireplace. A ceremonial pipe and a round ceramic container lay beside it. "I'd hoped you would come."

My gaze lingered on the tools. "A vision quest?"

His faded blue eyes swept over me. "You seek an answer that I can't give. Embrace the vision and learn from it."

I sat cross-legged on the floor and watched the man prepare the instrument. His stiff fingers fumbled with the lighter before the scent of sinsemilla filled the large room. He lifted the pipe and inhaled from it. He held onto the smoke for a few seconds, then passed the pipe to me.

When I turned sixteen, I took my first vision quest. Grandfather took me to a cabin up on Mount Alexa. We fasted for two days before entering a tent. I remember sweating and lots of hallucinations. A day later, I woke up at home. Grandfather told me that my spirit animal was a jaguar. It made its appearance that evening. I didn't recall whether weed was used during that journey.

Baba waved the pipe in front of me. If I wanted answers, I could either get them his way or do it on my own. If I stayed on my course, I'd only be tired and frustrated when the end arrived. Hesitantly, I put my lips on the device and inhaled.

"Close your eyes, Montezuma. Envision your dreams. Find your answers." The man chanted in his native tongue as my body relaxed and the spirit of the jaguar guided me.

A thick mist surrounds me.

When it parts, the gorgeous woman stands there. She runs a hand through her black wavy hair. "We finally meet."

"You're . . . Who are you?"

"An escort for Madame Death."

My heart falters a beat. "So, it's true? I'm going to die."

Her plump lips part. "One day, but not soon. I won't allow it."

I cock my head to one side. "I'm confused. If you work for Death, don't you have to do your job?"

"I don't work for Death. Unless you are of Asian descent, I won't be sent for you. Besides, I've been searching for you all my life." She steps closer and touches my face with her cold hand. "I have dreamed of you for years. It's Samhain. We must meet, but I don't know where to find you."

"A place called Havenwood Falls."

"I know of it."

The woman is astonishing. Her eyes are like brilliant green gems while her skin is so pale, it's almost transparent. I lean into her palm. "What's your name?"

18

"*Pandora.*" *She smiles, and I'm filled with warmth.* "*See you soon.*"

Before I can ask her anything else, the mist returns. The jaguar appears and nudges my hand.

"Montezuma."

I blinked and saw Baba staring at me.

"Did you find what you were seeking?"

"Not sure." I scrubbed my hand over my face. "The woman said she was an escort for Madame Death."

"Madame Death?" Baba parroted. He lowered his eyes, and his brow wrinkled. After a moment, he looked at me. "Japanese legend speaks of death spirits called shinigami. Essentially they're reapers, but aren't created by Death. They also behave a little differently."

"She said she wouldn't allow me to die. How is that possible? If she's one of these spirits, isn't her job collecting for Death?"

Baba gestured for me to help him up. After I assisted him, we walked out to the deck. The man gazed up into the sky and said, "I suspect that this female has a special connection with Death. Maybe she will utilize it to save you, Montezuma." He looked at me. "Go home and prepare yourself. I felt a sincere concern for your well-being just now. Sleep. Eat. Make peace with this life. Change is coming."

Humph. Yet another person suggesting a change was coming.

If that was true, would I like the person I'd become?

CHAPTER 4

PANDORA

I bolted upright in bed and ran a hand over my face. Whatever that was—vision or premonition—totally freaked me out. In all the years that I'd dreamed of the handsome stranger, we'd never spoken. I was grateful that we did, since it gave me a location for him. Too bad I didn't get a name.

I swung my feet to the floor and stared at it. Samhain was that evening. If I were going to Havenwood Falls, I had better hurry, especially since Death expected me to join him for—

My chirping phone stopped my thoughts. The only time it made that aggravating noise was when Madame Izanami summoned me. I accepted the call, thinking it would be my boss.

"Hello, Takara," the familiar voice rumbled through my device.

Shit! How did *he* get my number?

"H-hello."

"Am I disturbing you?"

"No." I slid out of bed and went straight to the closet for my suitcase. "I just woke up."

What should have been a quick trip was fast becoming a great escape. If I found what I was after, I didn't plan to return. If Death or Madame Izanami caught up with me, returning to the shadow realm would be the least of my concerns.

"Good. I'm looking forward to dinner this evening."

"About that . . ." I haphazardly grabbed outfits and tossed them onto the bed. "I'm not—"

"You're not denying your future husband, are you? I look forward to getting to know you before we are wed."

"And when is that exactly?"

"A week from today," he said with a hint of joy in his voice.

Nerves crawled through my gut. There was no way in hell (pun intended) I would marry Death. "I'm sorry, but I—"

"Need time?" The entity cleared his voice. "Very well, Takara. I will wait on you, but don't take too long. I expect you by my side in twenty-four hours."

I swallowed hard. "What happens then?"

"If you are not with me, I will be forced to send out my demon sentinels."

I envisioned demons hellbent on destruction, but were they worse than shinigami on a mission? What could happen?

They could end me . . .

Or Madame could evaporate me . . .

Or Death might come for me himself.

I was willing to chance it.

"Good to know. I'll see you soon," I lied.

Before Death disconnected the call, he added, "Oh, Takara, remember this."

"Yes?"

"I always get what I want, and my sentinels don't fail." On that note, he ended the call.

I tossed my phone onto the bed. Common sense dictated that I keep my ass in Yomi and prepare for a wedding. Problem was, I firmly believed that shinigami should have the possibility for love and happiness. If we could give it, we should be able to receive it too. And I wanted the opportunity.

Getting to the town hidden in a box canyon would be relatively easy. Death spirits only had to picture where we wanted to go, and we'd transport to our destination. Which was a good thing, since I needed to leave the realm without fanfare.

Zipping up my bag, I checked around the room, making sure I didn't forget anything. I'd left Hope a text message she'd receive upon waking. The female would be pissed because I didn't say exactly where

I was going. I had no choice but to keep her in the dark. If Madame summoned her, Hope couldn't be forced to divulge the information.

Minutes later, I stepped from the shadows and stood in a town square surrounded by quaint storefronts. Each one was decorated for Halloween—a big deal in a location full of supernaturals. It wasn't my first time in Havenwood Falls. Hope and I had an assignment there a few years ago. But it was my first occasion as a visitor. Which meant adhering to the guidelines protecting those who considered the town a safe haven.

Anticipating that a member of the Court of the Sun and the Moon would soon find me, I crossed the square and entered Whisper Falls Inn. It, too, was decked out for the holiday with cobwebs, pumpkins, skeletons, and decorative lights.

"Can I help you?" The voice was attached to a beautiful woman with amazing gray-green eyes. She had that distinct otherworldly fragrance.

Approaching the desk, I said, "I need a room if you have something available."

"For how long?"

Good question. How much time did I need to find the mystery man? "Maybe a couple of days?"

The woman peered over at a computer screen. "You're in luck. Your name?"

"Pandora."

Her fingers paused over the keyboard as she studied me. "Last name?"

"Just Pandora." I glanced over my shoulder and was grateful to see we were alone. I'd been in the woman's company long enough to detect that she was a moroi—a mortal vampire of Romanian ancestry. "And your name?"

"Michaela." Her eyebrows knitted together as if she picked up on something. Lowering her voice, she said, "Forgive me for saying it, but you're not human."

"No, and neither are you."

The woman crossed her arms. "Due to some trouble here, we've been scrutinizing everyone closer. What exactly are you, Pandora?"

"A death spirit," I murmured.

Her eyes widened as she leaned over the desk. "Is somebody about to die?"

"No. This is purely a visit. Call it a vacation."

Michaela pursed her shapely lips. "A reaper on vacation. That's a first."

"Reapers and shinigami aren't exactly the same. We have different employers and inhabit different realms. I primarily escort souls of Asian descent."

"So Death discriminates?"

I sighed. "Hey, I didn't make the rules. It's all based on a person's particular religion. If you're a follower of Shinto, you'll eventually see one of my kind."

Michaela gave me a hesitant nod like she wasn't quite convinced. "You'll need to register with the Court and get a temporary tattoo."

"I'm aware of that and have no issue with your rules. Anything else?" I tried hard to sound pleasant, but Michaela was starting to irk me. Discussing inane facts wasn't the best use of the little time I had.

"Since you know so much," she said in a snippy tone, "you won't mind staying put until my friend arrives. She'll do your ink and get you registered." Michaela pushed a key across the counter. "Your room is on the third floor."

Suddenly, it occurred to me that I had to smooth things out with the female. Otherwise, I was in for an unpleasant visit. Retrieving the key, I said, "I apologize for my bad behavior. This is an unsanctioned trip. The sooner I can find who I'm looking for, the sooner I can leave."

Michaela's icy attitude thawed. "Next time, lead with that. Addie Beaumont will be here as soon as she can. Care to tell me who you're looking for?"

"A man who rides a motorcycle and wears a leather jacket."

Michaela laughed.

"What's so funny?"

"You'll need more of a description than that. We have a motorcycle club in town. All the members of SIN wear leather."

"Oh." I hadn't considered that the jacket was part of a uniform. "He's tall and quite handsome."

"Still fits a lot of the members. Where did you meet this man?"

"That's the thing. I've only dreamed about him. Recently, his dream crossed over into mine."

She gasped. "You're the one."

"The one what?"

"I might know . . . Hang on." She pulled a phone from her jeans pocket. After a few minutes of viewing the screen, she turned the device toward me. "Is this him?"

Staring back at me was the stranger from my dreams—tall, slight build with dark hair and eyes. He was dressed in a black tuxedo. My heart stuttered when I considered the reason why his picture was on her phone. Hesitantly, I said, "Yes. And how do *you* know him?"

She smiled. "Monte and I are friends. I know his best friend's wife, Izzie. That picture was taken at the wedding."

Not convinced, I asked, "How did you know I was referring to him?"

"His friend, Hunter, told Izzie that Monte was having a hard time sleeping. She might have mentioned something about a dream to me on date night."

"Date night?"

Michaela returned the phone to her pocket. "My fiancé and I went out with Hunter and Izzie."

The joy of living in a small town. I sort of missed being in Yomi, where individuals minded their own business. *Most of the time.*

The door opened behind me and in walked a girl with a beanie covering her long dark hair. She carried two disposable cups in her hands. The rich smell of coffee tickled my nose as she came closer. "Michaela, I was coming out of Coffee Haven when I noticed—"

"Addie Beaumont, meet Pandora. She'll be—"

"Who died?" Her brown eyes widened behind a pair of black-framed glasses. "Please tell me—"

"No one's died," Michaela said. "Pandora's visit is—"

"Personal," I said.

I didn't want everyone knowing the reason I was in Havenwood Falls. This matter was between Monte and myself. Besides, there was a reaper in town—Shade StormIron—who worked for Death. It wouldn't be good for me if Shade reported back to his employer.

Addie blew air from her cheeks and placed the cups on the desktop. She patted the satchel strapped across her body. "Good thing

I carry this thing. Why don't we go to your room, Pandora? We can take care of a little business and have a discussion."

∾

The room assigned to me was quaint but comfortable—a suitable queen-sized bed with a floral covering, the standard chest of drawers and a dresser, a small sofa and matching chair.

Addie tested my blood sample, and then laid out her tools for the tattoo on the coffee table. "Can I ask a question?"

I leaned forward on the chair. "Does that count, or did you want to ask another one?"

She shot me a curious stare. "Did I say something to offend you?"

"No. I'm sorry, but I don't have a lot of time here. If my boss—"

"Death."

"No. *Madame* Death. Different entity. Different realm."

Addie held up a palm. "I get it. You want to hurry things along."

I nodded.

"As much as I can appreciate your predicament, I have to follow the rules. We've had some issues in town with unwanted *guests*, for lack of a better word, coming and going. Not following—"

"Say no more." I removed my jacket, leaving my arms bare. "This is a temporary design, right?"

"Yes."

The girl pulled out a sketchbook and pencil. "Any thoughts on what you'd like and where to put it?"

"A lit candle." I pointed to my shoulder.

Addie tilted her head to one side.

"It signifies the difference between shinigami and reapers. The latter harvest souls. shinigami escort. We make sure that people die when they're supposed to. A candle symbolizes our purpose. When the candle burns out, your time is up. We have no say in how fast or slow it burns."

"Interesting." She prepared her tattoo gun. "Actually, you clarified some things for me. Not too long ago I did a design for a reaper. How is it that you're not just a skeleton?"

"Another difference between shinigami and traditional reapers. We can maintain a corporeal form. It's a lot easier to help a soul cross over when they're not scared. We find this appearance more humane."

Addie shrugged. "I guess that makes sense."

"What will this tattoo do for me besides track me like supernatural GPS?"

The girl smiled. "You'll feel more human and have basic human needs."

"Like?"

"Eating, sleeping . . ." She tucked a strand of hair behind an ear. "Desires."

I arched an eyebrow. "But I already have those things."

"But do you always act on them? What about the desires?"

Without explaining myself, I said, "You're right."

As Addie prepped my skin with a wipe, she asked, "So tell me, if you're not here on a mission, what brings you to Havenwood Falls?"

I reminded myself that she wasn't my enemy. News of the Collector traveled as far as Yomi. We knew of the turmoil the being created in town. If the havoc had happened in my realm, we would've been just as cautious. "I'm seeking someone I've being dreaming of for a century."

"That's a long time to have the same dream. Do you know who it is?"

"Thanks to Michaela I do." I flinched as the needle touched my flesh. "Where do I find SIN?"

Addie chuckled. "You mean the MC clubhouse? It's about a block south from here, off Tenth Street and Petran. Are you sure you want to go there? It's not the most savory of places."

"That doesn't matter. My curiosity won't let me rest until I find Monte."

Addie finished up her design with a huge grin on her face. "You're looking for Monte? I could ask around for you. Find out where he might be."

"Thank you." I touched her forearm. "I really do apologize for my rudeness. I'm normally polite, but—"

"Understood. But why the rush?"

"I'm supposed to meet him tonight." I shrugged on my jacket and stood. "Madame Death doesn't know where I am. Making matters worse, Death will be looking for me too."

Addie shuddered. "I don't envy you. Whatever happens, Death can't come to Havenwood Falls." She gathered her gear and then added in a less stern voice, "That reaper I mentioned is still in town. Maybe he can be of some help."

"How can Shade help me?"

"He might know where his employer is," Addie offered.

"If the need arises, I'll find the reaper. For now, can we just go to Monte's?" I had no intention of upsetting his timeline. I just wanted to see where he lived so that I could find him later.

She closed up her bag. "Just a warning. Monte Tayute is one of the good guys. A lot of people in Havenwood Falls like him. If you're here to hurt him . . ."

"I have no intentions of doing so." Far from it. I hoped Monte would be my key to some long overdue happiness.

CHAPTER 5

MONTE

*D*espite Baba's suggestion that I go home and prepare for what's coming, I couldn't do it. Senora's words made a lot more sense. I should fight for my life. Nobody else was going to do it. If my father was around, he'd say the same thing. Right after he called me a fucking idiot for believing a shaman—Dad didn't embrace certain facets of our heritage. So instead of following directions, I decided to seek out advice from someone who should know.

I walked through the door of the Dirty Knuckle and scanned the room. It was still early enough for the place to be relatively empty. The being I searched for—taut physique shoved into a pair of jeans, snug T-shirt, leather jacket, and Timberland boots—sat at the bar. When he turned his scruffy face toward me, I knew I'd found the reaper known as Shade.

Rhys Graywalk, the owner and a member of the fae species, waved as I approached. "What can I get you, Monte?"

"Whatever he's having." I jerked my head toward Shade. "Make it two."

Shade smiled. "Thanks. Something tells me you're not just being generous, though."

I sat on a barstool and took the bottle of beer from Rhys. "I'm glad you're still in town."

"Part of the reprieve from my employer. What do you need from me?"

"You can tell when there's a soul to be reaped, right?" I lifted the bottle to my lips.

"Yup. Clear as a bell." His gaze raked over me. "You think I'm here for you?"

"Are you?"

"No."

"Maybe one of your coworkers?"

Shade's lips flattened as he shook his head. "Why the concern?"

"A shaman said my time might be up." Sharing the intricacies of Baba's vision wasn't necessary. "Just looking for confirmation."

The reaper chuckled and picked up his beer. "You might want to see what he's been smoking. If your time was up, I'd know it."

Senora's theory gained more validity. The dream wasn't a warning of doom after all.

"Another question?"

"Shoot."

"Ever hear of Madame Death?"

Shade snorted. "Yeah, but she doesn't work for my boss. Her name's actually Izanami. She dwells in the Japanese underworld. Nobody for you to worry about unless you have some Asian blood."

"Naw. I'm Maya. Trust me, we have enough troublesome evil deities." I paused for a moment as a couple of humans walked by. When they left, I continued, "Any idea why a Japanese reaper is haunting my dreams?"

"Hell if I know. No pun intended. Maybe she's curious about this world." He shoved to his feet and reached for his wallet. "Catch you around."

Rhys made his way back over to me. "Discover what you're looking for?"

"Not really. Got more questions if anything." I pulled out a few bills and handed them over. "Problem is, I don't know where to get the answers."

He placed his elbows on the bar and leaned in. "Listen, I don't know your troubles, and I'm not trying to get into your business, but I overheard your discussion. Tonight's Samhain. Maybe your answers will come with it. If not, it wouldn't hurt to pay Teeny or even Eloise Sinclair a visit. A psychic reading might help."

"Maybe. Have a good night."

~

The trick-or-treaters kept me busy. Each time I sat down to enjoy my pizza from Napoli's, the doorbell rang. After an hour of running back and forth, I was ready for a little downtime. Despite the voice of reason telling me not to do it, I threw caution to the wind, hopped on my bike, and went for a ride. Normally, if I'd had a few beers, I didn't drive, but that night I said fuck it. Yes, I was tempting fate, but I'd rather meet my fate head on than hide from it. The road was clear as I came around the bend, heading toward the Welcome sign.

It was unusually quiet, but that was a good thing. My mind cleared for the first time in days as I savored the cool breeze. Contentment was the best way to describe how I felt, and I put aside the worries Baba tried to implant.

A few more miles, then I'd turn around and go home. Maybe I'd have an easier time falling asleep.

What the fuck?!

My front tire hit a slick spot in the road. I tried staying calm. Nine times out of ten, the bike would make the correction itself. I decelerated, but the usual maneuvers didn't work. I crashed onto the side of the road. Lying on my back, I glanced around. Nothing but hazy darkness greeted me. I was dazed but not seriously hurt. Then I heard the sound—bullets punching the asphalt.

I blinked a few times as reality set in—my dream. My vision cleared as a pair of high heels came into view. My gaze traveled up a shapely leg clad in black leather.

She was gorgeous, with wavy onyx-colored hair that hung to her tiny waist. Her curves grabbed my attention better than any mountain road. A pair of jade-green eyes stared down at me. Time stopped as something foreign tugged at my heart. An overwhelming sense of peace mixed with desire hit me. If this was dying, I'd succumb to it.

"Not tonight," said a voice like that of an angel whispering. "It's not your time."

For a minute, I was lost. According to Baba, the dream was a premonition of my impending death, but I felt very much alive. My stiffening dick confirmed it. "Who are you?"

"Pandora. Let's get you back on your feet."

I knew that name. It hit me harder than the asphalt did. She was the being from my dream.

The woman helped me raise my bike off the pavement. I brushed the leaves and dirt off my ass while my brain struggled to make sense of what happened.

Her bright red lips curled up, and she tossed an elegant leg over the bike seat. "Monte, how about we get you back home?"

Still stunned, I asked, "You ride?"

"It's been a while, but I remember how. Besides, I don't think you're in any shape to drive." She passed me my helmet. "I'm guessing this fell off."

Sluggishly, I got on the bike behind Pandora. It felt strange letting someone else do the driving, but my head still rang from the fall. Maybe it was all just another dream. I could just sit back and let go.

Within minutes, Pandora had parked the bike in my driveway. How did she know where I lived? Maybe knowledge came with the dream? Pandora let me lean on her, awkward given our height difference, as we walked toward the front door. Instead of waiting for permission, she unlocked it and ushered me to the sofa.

"Is there someone you want me to call? Someone to make sure you're okay?" Her muffled voice came from someplace beside me.

"Huh?" My head throbbed badly.

Her cool hand stroked my forehead. "I don't know a lot about shifters, but I suspect you have a concussion. Where do you keep your aspirin?"

I simply looked at her.

"Never mind. I'll find it myself."

Someone shook my shoulder, stirring me from sleep. I cracked open my eyes and squinted around the room. My gaze landed on a lovely woman. Slowly, I pushed up on my elbows. "It wasn't a dream."

"No." She held out a glass of water and two pills. "Take these."

I did.

"Do you remember what happened?"

"I laid down my bike." My mind was fuzzy, but I was pretty sure nobody else was involved in the wreck.

"Yes. I found you on the side of the road. Your helmet flew off, so I think you may have hit your head." Her leather creaked as she stood. "Do you remember my name?"

"Pandora."

"Right."

"What the hell are you?"

"Interesting choice of words." She perched on the edge of the recliner, crossed her legs, and anchored her gaze on me. "Forgive me for staring, but I never imagined we'd meet outside of my dreams."

Despite the overwhelming pain, I sat taller. "You've dreamed of me?"

"For a hundred years I've had the same dream. I've watched you spin out on that road a thousand times or more."

None of that made sense to my addled brain. I had limited experience around reapers. I didn't think soldiers of death had conversations with their targets before carting them away.

Her foot bobbed to some beat only she could hear. "Maybe I should clarify myself. Right now, you're confused, thinking I've come for your soul. Totally wrong. My visit here is purely personal."

My eyebrows knitted together—even that hurt. "A reaper with an agenda?"

Pandora frowned. "Not a reaper. Ever hear of shinigami?"

Slowly Shade's words came back to me. *Madame Death . . . Izanami . . . Japanese underworld . . .* "You don't work for Death, right?"

"Correct."

"So, where am I headed?"

"Oh, Monte." She sighed. "I'm not here for you in the traditional sense."

Beads of cold sweat trickled down my spine. "How then?"

She blew air through her cheeks. "Apparently everything you've heard about my kind is wrong." Pandora lowered her leg and leaned forward. "There are shinigami who work just like traditional reapers. Some of them can be quite violent in their endeavors. I, on the other hand, work in a more peaceful branch of the Japanese underworld.

I'm more of an angel who escorts souls to their afterlife. But, Monte, it's not your time yet. No one is taking you anywhere that you don't want to go."

"Then why invade my dreams?"

Pandora smiled. "Did you know that shinigami are denied pleasure? As an escort, I use pleasure to guide my marks, but I don't get to enjoy it. Can you imagine existing like that?"

I noticed that she avoided my question.

"No," I said quietly. It was one thing to deny yourself ecstasy. It was something entirely different when you weren't allowed it because of some restriction. "Why?"

"Madame Death says that it interferes with our jobs." Pandora's shoulders slumped. "She believes that emotions make us less effective."

Putting two and two together, I said flatly, "Is that why you're here? Looking for a good time?"

So the death spirit came to me to get her freak on? Flattering as fuck, but . . .

Yeah, yeah, I hadn't gotten laid in a while, but hooking up with a harvester? I had a hard time wrapping my head around the idea. After all, she was an entity who dealt in death.

It wasn't like I had an issue with folks dying. Shit, I'd seen my fair share as a member of SIN, but it didn't mean I condoned it. And I sure as hell wasn't thinking about getting sideways with a spirit.

Squeaking, like leather rubbing against itself, snagged my attention. Pandora stood and removed her jacket. Underneath it was a garment that could only be called lingerie—her ample boobs spilled over the top of the sleeveless item.

Damn. Getting sideways might not be a bad thing.

My dick twitched, agreeing with me. Pandora wasn't there to take me to Hell. She wanted to take me to paradise. Would it be worth the trip?

The sofa cushion dipped as she sat beside me. Her cool breath chilled my cheek as she leaned in. "I'm just asking to be indulged. I want to feel passion for a change. I chose you, Monte, because I can't stop dreaming of you."

Her lips brushed my ear, and goosebumps rose on my skin. I drew in a breath.

Pandora glanced down at my swollen crotch. "You can't deny that you're interested."

"But I—"

"Kiss me." She placed a hand on my face and turned me toward her. "Just a kiss. Let's find out if there was anything to those dreams."

Be careful, said the voice of reason.

Death delivered by kiss. For all I knew, it was how her kind worked. But deep down, I wanted to know what those dreams meant.

I cupped Pandora's head and kissed those sumptuous lips. Her touch was cool, but her mouth was warm and welcoming. The peace I felt earlier morphed into something more like bliss. Pure, unadulterated bliss that erased the pain in my head as my heart kicked out its own joyful beat. I leaned back, bringing the voluptuous woman on top of me. A lusty feeling ignited inside my body, and I didn't want to fight it.

She moaned and dragged her lips from mine. "Still want to question why I'm here?"

I gripped her ass and pulled her closer. "No. One other question?"

"What?"

"Do I need a condom?"

Pandora laughed. "I'm a spirit. We don't get sick or diseased."

"All I needed to know."

She dragged me to my feet. "I have a question. Where's your bed?"

"Upstairs." I growled. "Now."

CHAPTER 6

PANDORA

*H*e didn't have to say it twice. I jumped to my feet and raced him to the stairs. We took them at a mad pace until we reached the bedroom. Monte moved past me and sat on the edge of a hand-carved king-size bed. From the headboard down to the posts were intricate designs of outdoor scenes featuring jaguars. It made sense, since he was a nagual shifter. He ran his hand over the silky sheets and then tapped the mattress.

"Shouldn't I get undressed?" I asked coyly, as I stopped in the center of the room and gazed at the Aztec-patterned throw rug near the bed. A trunk with a brightly colored blanket sat beneath a window overlooking the street.

"Can you leave on the . . . um . . . ." His finger moved up and down over my corset.

"I can."

"And the shoes. Please leave those on." The request was rough-voiced and so damned sexy.

I snapped my fingers, and my leather pants vanished. Normally, I enjoyed the process of getting dressed and undressed. It made me feel more human, but in that moment what I wanted to feel was a lot more than humanity.

Monte sighed deeply as his eyes swept over me.

I sashayed closer. "You're overdressed."

He reached behind him and yanked off his T-shirt, then leaned back on the bed.

I licked my lips, longing to touch his bare chest. Not wasting a minute, I crawled up beside Monte, planting kisses across his sculpted abs. When I reached the waistband of his jeans, my fingers moved over his zipper, massaging his crotch. He sighed again, and I continued my mission as he lifted his hips. With a bit of a tug, I dragged the garment over his muscular thighs.

I glanced up, ready to remove his underwear, and drew in a breath. There were none. I bit my lip and stared at his magnificent stiff cock. It would have made Michelangelo's David envious. As it twitched, I wanted nothing more than to taste him—run my tongue along the taut skin and . . . Wrapping my hand around the stiff base, I lowered my head.

"Oh, fuck . . ."

My mouth worshipped Monte as if his dick was an altar, and I was an eager devotee. When I flattened my tongue over the sensitive tip, his body bucked repeatedly. I thought he was about to explode when I felt his hands on my shoulders.

"Pan . . . Pandora, stop," he panted.

I lifted my head, disappointed that he didn't want more.

He shifted to his knees and gestured for me to lie down. "You said you wanted to experience pleasure. Let me."

I stretched out on the bed. Odd. The sheets felt cool against my back. I never noticed changes in temperature before.

Monte ran his fingers up my thighs, caressing the skin, and parted my knees. He made a hungry sound in the back of his throat as his hand slid between my legs and stroked the spot no man had ever touched. I gasped, and my entire body vibrated in response.

The sound of fabric ripping filled the silence as Monte yanked off my lace thong. He dropped his head and explored me with his tongue. That clever instrument set off a blinding, surprising heat within me. I shut my eyes and luxuriated in that sweet sensation for a moment. It sizzled through every part of my body—exhilarating and captivating. Something built within me. My body bowed. My toes curled. I'd never seen Heaven, but if it felt like that . . . The sensation started like a ripple and grew and grew until I was tumbling through the ether.

"Monte!"

Incoherent sounds spilled from my mouth as I convulsed uncontrollably. Then Monte's lips claimed mine—the taste of myself thick on his tongue. The wave petered out as I lost myself in his kiss, but my throbbing pussy reminded me that the task was only half done.

He rolled onto his back, bringing me with him. I straddled him, lowering myself little by little over his twitching dick.

He exhaled and with one quick thrust pressed into me. For a moment, I remained still—appreciating how he filled me. His enormity stretched me, but there wasn't any pain. Shinigami didn't feel it. Instead, I was mesmerized that every inch of him fit.

Slowly, I rotated my hips and we moved as one. He ran his hands over my hips and up my back. My entire body tingled from his touch while his rigid shaft stroked me. He felt . . .

Amazing.

I closed my eyes as Monte pulled me into him. His lips were on mine again.

"Look at me," he demanded. "I want to see you come."

I honored his request, all the while gyrating and grinding atop him. With each thrust from Monte, that newly found pleasure racked my body. He hammered into me—a rush of pure need from him.

Eyes locked. Body to body. We moved.

Passion took over, and we quivered—gasping and groaning—together.

Later, lying in Monte's strong arms, I purred like a kitten as he stroked my backside and kissed my temple. I'd never experienced passion or an orgasm, but I was so happy it was with that man.

"Are you okay?"

"Better than okay." I couldn't help but tease him. "What about you? Still alive?"

He laughed. "Very much so."

From his stiffening dick against my thigh, I was assured that he hadn't crossed over.

"Tell me something, Pandora. You said that you'd never enjoyed sex, but you seemed to enjoy it just now. How is that possible?"

Valid question worthy of a good answer. I only had speculation. "Maybe because I chose you?"

"I don't understand."

"Madame Death wished for shinigami to interact with the modern world more efficiently, so she created an escort service. We cater mostly to humans and supernaturals of Asian descent. The headquarters is in Tokyo, and we have an app on cell phones."

"Like Tinder?" When I didn't respond, he added, "Human dating service app. It allows them to find possible matches for dates."

I thought about it for a moment. "Very similar. The escort service piggybacks on real services."

"I don't follow."

I sat up and pulled the sheet higher over my breasts. "The escort service issues death cards for marks. We use technology to monitor dating services like Tinder. If a request is found for someone who is on a card—"

"Shinigami Escorts intervenes."

"Right. We never choose our targets. Each one is merely an assignment for us. Maybe because you're not on anyone's death card and not a job for me, I get to feel."

Monte rubbed the tattoo on my shoulder. "Addie's creation?"

"Yes." The candle with a faint image of bones in the base and a flame made to look like a clock on fire was true artistry. "That might have something to do with it too." I glanced at him. "Does it matter to you? Isn't it enough that you gave me pleasure?"

A crooked grin crossed his handsome face. "I'm not arguing. I just wonder what the fuck's next."

I leaned in and kissed him. "What's next should take us to sunrise. That is, if you're up for it."

He moved closer, forcing me onto my back. "Oh, I'm definitely up for more of you."

Bright sunshine, filtering through the curtains, hit me in the face as I woke up. It took me a minute to realize that I wasn't in the shadowy realm. Rolling over, I noticed Monte was gone, but there was a fresh T-shirt beside me. I slipped it on, and it swallowed me. The hem hung past my knees while the edge of the sleeves hit my forearms, but it smelled like him—woodsy with a hint of musk. I went to the window and looked out. I'd never seen a sunny day before—the escort service normally sent death spirits out in the evening. It was absolutely beautiful outside with the sun rays glistening off the orange and red leaves.

"Good morning." Monte's voice came from the doorway.

I whirled around and smiled. The man was gorgeous even in flannel pajama bottoms. I loved the scruffy appearance, but he was so much taller than I'd imagined. I was around five feet seven, but Monte had another eight inches on me.

"Good morning to you," I said.

"I didn't know if you ate." He held up a tray of food—toast, bacon, eggs, and a carafe of orange juice. Two steaming mugs were on it as well.

"Definitely!" I hurried over to him. "Remember, I'm not a reaper. Shinigami eat and sleep. We just don't enjoy sex." I winked. "Usually."

Monte set the tray onto the bed and sat down. "How long before you have to go back?"

A valid question that I didn't want to ponder. "Why don't we take it day by day? See how it goes?"

"Won't your employer be looking for you?" He spread marmalade on a triangle of toast.

"I'm sure Madame Death is doing that as we speak." Frankly, I was less worried about her than about Death. I was in a hell of a lot of trouble.

Monte handed me a plate and a fork. "Can I be honest with you?"

"Always." I began eating. The food was very good.

"I'd like it if you'd stay. With me, that is."

"Oh?" Suddenly, I felt the sorrow weighing on him like a stone. I dropped my utensil. "What's wrong?"

He swallowed hard. "Until you arrived, I thought I was dying. It was the only change in an otherwise dull life."

"How so?"

"Pandora, I live alone and work in a garage. When I'm not there, I'm at the clubhouse with the MC. Ask anyone in town, and they can tell you what I do any day of the week."

I touched his leg. "Why do you choose to live like that?"

"It's easier." He took a sip from the mug. "Growing up, I got in a hell of a lot of trouble with the government. I was just a kid, but officials don't care about age when secure computers are hacked."

"They must not have been too secure if a child could get into them."

He nodded. "They didn't see it that way. I was facing prosecution. Thankfully, my grandparents were in town. They brought me to Havenwood Falls."

"Have you seen your parents since you came here?"

"No. A year after I left, they moved, and I got a letter from them. We haven't seen each other since I was fourteen. We communicate once a month through the darknet."

"It sounds like Havenwood Falls is more of a prison than a haven for you."

He shook his head. "No fucking way. My best friend is here. I have brothers with the MC. As long as I stay close to town, I'm good."

I squinted at Monte. "That doesn't mean you have to live alone."

"I know, but I hadn't met anyone in a long time that interested me." He lowered his head. "Until you."

Sorry, I wasn't buying it. There had to be more to Monte's story. How could he live in a place full of supes and not find a suitable mate?

Maybe he was waiting for you.

That wasn't a logical answer. For all he knew, I was a figment of his imagination that entered his dream state. Nothing more. Hopefully, there'd be time to unravel his mysteries. Until my employer—or Death himself—caught up with me, I planned on enjoying every single moment with Monte.

CHAPTER 7

MONTE

*I*t had been a long time since I awakened with a woman in my bed. Recalling the undeniable chemistry between us and having Pandora next to me shone a bright light on just how lonely I was. Hell, if someone like Savage could find someone, what the fuck was wrong with me?

Small talk was not normal for me after sex, but the female captivating my thoughts made me want to know everything and anything about her. Reaching out, I ran my fingers over Pandora's leg. Just making sure she was real.

"You have someplace to be this morning?" I asked, hoping that I was her only reason for being in town. For all I knew, it could be the truth, since we never finished our discussion the previous night.

She gazed up at me through her long lashes as if I was her entire world. I'd be lying if I said that small gesture didn't fucking make my heart beat faster and harden my dick.

Her plump lips curled up. "Not at the moment."

Suddenly, I wanted to be buried deep inside of her again. Frankly, nothing else vied for my attention. As far as I was concerned, I was in the only place that mattered. I took the tray, still full of food, and set it on the floor.

"I thought you were hungry," Pandora said.

"I am." My eyes caressed her curvaceous body, and despite the lust burning in my brain, I had to ask, "How are you a spirit? I can touch and see you . . . Feel you too."

Pandora moved to her knees and cupped my face between her dainty hands. "Peaceful escorts are meant to entice. Don't you think it would be hard to do so as a skeleton?"

"Yeah, but . . . You're just like I dreamed."

Pandora nodded. "That I can't explain. Maybe our dreams crossed?"

"How?"

Her eyes met mine. "Do you really want to spend time pondering how and why I exist?"

"No." I leaned in and kissed her. My hands slid around Pandora's back and rested on her ample ass. Lifting her, I pulled her closer. "I'd rather do this . . ." I kissed her again. "And this . . ." I nuzzled her neck. "Matter of fact, we're not leaving this bed today."

She giggled as she ran her fingernails over my scalp. "Like I said, I aim to please."

Half an hour later, we lay beside each other panting. My heart ricocheted in my chest, but for a change it wasn't anxiety. The palpitations were courtesy of the beauty in my bed. Call me foolish, but I was afraid to speak, thinking that my voice would shatter the illusion, and once again, I'd be alone. A soft chirping, however, interrupted the moment.

"What's that?" I sat up and glanced around the room.

Pandora touched my arm. "It's just my phone. Ignore it."

"Uh . . . no." I wasn't in the habit of not answering phones. People got hurt. Loved ones died. I didn't want that on my conscience. I tossed back the covers and saw her device on the floor.

When I reached for it, Pandora shouted, "Don't touch it!"

I stared at the device until it stopped ringing. Looking over my shoulder, I asked, "What's going on?"

Her gaze flicked to the ceiling. Shutting her eyes, Pandora said, "It was just my roommate, Hope. No big deal."

"What if she needed you?" Concern colored my tone. My mind

always formulated worst-case scenarios. It was a lingering tendency from my past. "She could be in trouble."

"Trust me, she's not. If anyone's in trouble, it's me." Pandora glanced at me.

"Why?" My heart froze. What the fuck had I gotten myself into?

A hot-as-hell female that makes you feel good, that's what.

She plastered on a smile and slid onto my lap. "It's nothing for you to worry about. I'll handle it later."

"Later?" I squinted at her as reality set in. "You're not staying?"

Pandora's arms snaked over my shoulders. "Let's not talk about that now. We're having fun . . ."

Granted, my life needed to change. I'd sat on the sidelines letting everyone else have fun while I lived like a goddamned monk.

You were protecting your heart.

Wrong. I was being a coward. That fucked-up existence was over. What I didn't need, though, was someone else's drama. Maybe it was best to end things before I let my heart get entangled, so I pulled out of Pandora's grasp and lifted her off of me. Talking took me out of the mood, anyway.

My damned heart, however, didn't want to let go. It wanted more than a quick fuck with Pandora. Frankly, if all I wanted was to get my dick stroked, I could have found anyone in town to do the job. It wasn't like I didn't get offers.

She frowned. "What's wrong?"

"Bathroom's down the hall," I said, forcing indifference into my voice. "Clean towels are beneath the sink. After you're dressed, I'll drop you off wherever you want."

Her lips trembled as her eyes—like bright marbles—popped wide. "We're finished?"

I raked a hand through my unkempt, dark hair. "Just because I'm a biker doesn't mean I'm not an honest man. Either tell me the fucking truth or we're done. I don't have time for someone looking to fulfill some damned fantasy."

"But—"

"But if you came looking for something real, then you have to be straight with me." I blew air through my cheeks, realizing I was a hypocrite. "I'd like to get to know you, not just for sex."

Pandora remained silent. The walls began closing in around me, and I couldn't stand being in her presence any longer. If she was leaving, I wanted to get used to the solitude as soon as possible. I stood, stalked over to the chest in the corner, and pulled a pair of jeans and a T-shirt from a drawer. As I dressed, I heard the bedroom door open and close.

∾

Much later, I parked my bike in Hunter's driveway. Pandora didn't take me up on my offer. When I left the bedroom, she was gone. I suspected she was staying at Whisper Falls Inn, but I wouldn't go there. I might check after I spoke to Hunter.

Baba let me in and said that Hunter was in the great room. I found him in front of the fireplace, stoking the flames. When I dropped onto the sofa, he glanced up.

"Man, you look like shit. Get up on the wrong side of the bed?" He replaced the poker and sat beside me. Hunter picked up a burgundy coffee mug from the low table. "You want some?"

"Only if you're adding bourbon."

"Damn. Is it that bad?"

I closed my eyes and leaned my head against the back of the sofa. "I met someone."

"Uh-oh." He remained quiet for a long, uncomfortable minute. "Is she married?"

Cracking open an eye, I glared at Hunter. "Did you forget who you're talking to? Married females are more your style."

He chuckled. "Used to be." He held up his left hand and flashed the wedding band. "If you didn't hook up with someone already spoken for, what's the problem?"

"Lack of honesty."

"Aw, man." Hunter stood. "I need a refill for this conversation. Give me a minute."

Instead of waiting, I followed him into the kitchen and grabbed a cup from the cabinet. I leaned against the counter while my friend poured.

"Let me get this straight. You just met a woman, and you hit her with the let's-be-totally-honest speech? How many times—"

I loved Hunter like a brother, but my attitude with women was a sore point between us. Before Izzie, my friend was a fuck 'em and leave 'em kind of guy. Me? I was the odd duck, not fucking around and caring about the female afterward. At one point, Hunter thought I was gay. He claimed I had too many fucking emotions. Plus, I wanted the perfect girl in my life. Those things made me an unlikely candidate to join SIN. Thankfully, Liam and the guys saw past all that. I was an asset—an unexpected one.

"Not how it happened," I clarified.

Hunter ignored me. "You know that shit only plays with . . . Fuck, did you meet your soul mate?"

I blew on the coffee and took a sip. "She doesn't have a soul."

Hunter's eyes widened. "You hooked up with a vampire?"

"No."

Lowering his voice, he said, "Please tell me you didn't fuck Senora."

"Nope, I haven't laid a finger—" I wasn't even remotely interested in the empusa—not counting my near slip-up at the party the other day. There was no denying that she was attractive, but I preferred females who wouldn't snack on me after sex. "Why would you think that?"

"Just saying. I saw you two talking at the clubhouse party."

"Only talking." I stared down at the coffee. In order to drink the sludge Hunter prepared, I had to cut it with something. "Got any creamer?"

"Check the fridge. Izzie's fond of some new flavored shit." His face scrunched up. "Tastes like pumpkin pie."

I laughed. Hunter was one of the few people I knew who hated the dessert. I, on the other hand, loved it. Opening the refrigerator, I found the carton and added a generous portion to my cup. Not even bothering to stir, I tasted it. Much better.

"So who did you meet without a soul?"

Lowering the mug, I said, "Ever hear of shinigami?"

Hunter shook his head.

"In a nutshell, she's like a reaper, but she only works in the Japanese shadow realm."

"How did you fucking meet her?" Hunter opened a plastic container and offered me some brownies.

I started to take one but hesitated. "Did Baba make these?"

Hunter waggled his eyebrows. "His specialty."

"I'll pass."

"I thought since you were hanging out at Circle J—"

"It was a one-time thing." I topped off my coffee. "Can we get back to my—"

"What's the problem? Was she a dud in bed?"

"Far from it." Memories of my time with Pandora put a smile on my face. "She got a phone call this morning."

"Oh hell, that's never good. Let me guess. She has a boyfriend."

I gave Hunter a pointed look.

He lifted his palms. "Sorry."

Ever since he married Izzie, my friend had taken on the role of analyzing the shit out of everyone

"Pandora didn't answer the phone. When I asked her about it, she said it was her roommate."

"You don't believe her?" His eyebrows touched. "Pandora . . . If my memory is correct, wasn't that the chick in Greek mythology who fucked up and opened a jar of evil? Maybe it's best to kick that problem to the curb."

I shrugged. "Not that easy. I want to believe her."

Hunter leaned against the counter. "What's stopping you?"

"Her employer."

"Why would Death care?"

"Pandora doesn't work for Death. Different entity. She called her employer Madame Death."

Hunter returned the pot brownies to the cabinet, and then placed his empty mug in the sink. "You're losing me, Monte. Why would it matter if Death, Madame Death, or Jehoshaphat himself knew where this shinigami is? How does that affect *you* having a good time?"

"I told Pandora I wanted more than a quick fuck."

"Then have *several* quick fucks!" Exasperated, he rubbed at his eyelid. "She's not your soul mate. You have no obligation other than pure enjoyment. Brother, you've got an enviable situation."

"What's so enviable?" Izzie's voice floated into the room.

Hunter opened his arms when the lovely shifter strolled up to him. "*Cariño*, I only have eyes for you."

She hit his chest. Keeping her eyes on him, she said to me, "It's good to see you, Monte. Staying for brunch? I could whip up something."

"That's okay." I wasn't just being polite. Hunter and his grandfather were the chefs in their household. My friend frequently joked that Izzie could burn water. "I've got something to take care of."

Hunter wrapped his arms around his wife and said, "Off to work?"

"Naw. Going to fix something else I broke."

I didn't see my situation through Hunter's eyes. I'd never been one to crave sex without an attachment, even though I'd met plenty of women who relished the status. I was a man who wanted the commitment.

CHAPTER 8

PANDORA

I should have had my head examined thinking I could enter the human world and satisfy my desires. Full lives weren't possible for shinigami. We had one purpose in the world, and spending time with someone who made me feel good wasn't it.

Truly, I wanted to do my job and not cause trouble. But I didn't understand why it had to be so cut and dried. There were so many blasted rules surrounding my race of beings. We couldn't marry. We couldn't have offspring. We couldn't enjoy sex. Hell, we couldn't indulge in it unless it was an assignment. The way I saw it, we were a race banned from happiness.

In the end, I supposed it didn't matter. Between Madame Izanami and Death, I'd eventually be found. If my employer located me, there'd be a lengthy lecture before she unraveled me. But my husband-to-be would keep me from banishment to the shadows. Instead, I'd walk down the aisle. In any case, I was doomed.

Thinking about an eternity as the bride of Death was disturbing. Destiny was fucking with me. Snuggling up to a cold entity each night wasn't acceptable.

Not after Monte.

As I slammed my suitcase closed, my phone rang, and I picked it up without checking the screen—something I rarely did. "Hello?"

"Pandora, it's me."

The sound of my partner's frantic voice gave me pause. I'd forgotten to contact her.

"Hope." I plopped down on the bed and slipped my feet into my heels. "I'm so sorry I didn't return your call."

"You don't have time for apologies," she admonished. "You need to hurry and get your ass back in Yomi."

"Let me guess," I said flippantly. "Madame's looking for me?"

"Of course, and she's pissed, but your problem is with Death. The entity is coming for you."

"I figured he would eventually, but how did you know he was coming?"

Hope breathed heavily into the phone. "Death showed up at our apartment again. After he left, I went to Izanami for some info. That promise Death mentioned? She agreed to an arrangement with him when you were created."

"Fuck no!" I hadn't considered that Madame had set up the walk-down-the-aisle moment.

"Pandora."

I wouldn't become the bride of Death. Maybe if I refused, I'd only have to endure Izanami's punishment.

It will not come from Madame Death.

True, but fucking Death—a cold, heartless lover—every night would be a punishment too.

"She should have consulted me."

"You know that's not how things are done in our world." Hope paused for a moment. "Pandora, I don't see how you have a choice."

Shinigami didn't get a say in how we existed or in what assignments we took. It was the prevailing reason Madame used for not giving us hearts and souls, but when it came to me, somebody goofed. I felt something beating erratically in my chest.

"I don't—" Someone knocked on my door. "Hope, I'll contact you when I can. For now, if Izanami asks, just tell her I'm still in Japan."

"I'll do no such thing. I happen to like *my* existence." She disconnected the call.

Tossing my phone aside, I dragged my feet across the room. Nobody knew I was there other than Michaela and Addie. I stood with my hand on the knob. "Who is it?"

"Monte."

What the hell? I yanked the door open. Instead of being cordial, I lit into him. "What do you want?"

He leaned his tall frame against the wall and gazed at me with hooded eyes. "I just want to talk. We can go somewhere else." He jerked his head toward the steps. "There's a bar downstairs."

Honestly, I didn't want anyone else listening in on our conversation. With our chemistry, it was dangerous being alone with him, but I'd chance it. I stepped to one side and allowed him to enter. Closing the door, I rested my head against the wood, trying to summon strength.

"Pandora."

Monte's pleading voice snagged my attention, and I faced him. Searching for a reason to speak, I settled on gratitude. "I should thank you for last night. You allowed me to feel what I'd never been able—"

Before I could finish my thought, Monte's rough lips claimed mine. It was a hungry kiss full of passion and desperation. I moaned as he lifted me into his strong arms. The next thing I felt was the soft bed against my back. No, I couldn't allow . . . He said he wanted to talk . . .

"Monte, no," I complained.

"Give in." He reached for my feet and removed my shoes.

Resist him, my brain said, while another part of me wanted him to keep going. "I-I—"

Monte knocked my suitcase to the floor. His gaze met mine, and then he yanked my pants off. Unzipping his jeans, he uttered, "Get something straight. I'm going to fuck you, and then we talk. Only truth between us, Pandora, or I walk out of here."

His commanding tone, bordering on arrogance, was damned sexy. But always a smart ass, I countered, "How about *I* fuck you? When *I'm* done, you're welcome to walk out of here. No words necessary."

A low rumble came from Monte as he spread my legs wide, pushed my panties aside, and plunged his thick cock deep inside of me. I gasped.

"Too late. I'm. Fucking. You." Each word was punctuated with a well-placed thrust.

Damn. I wanted to say something, but my voice was lost. A crescendo of emotions hit me all at once, and then my toes curled . . .

My hips lifted . . . I gritted my teeth as strong vibrations swept through me. The bed creaked beneath us, and the headboard slammed into the wall. We were so fucking loud I was surprised nobody knocked on the door. Monte came with a shuddering cry. I buried my face in his chest—slightly embarrassed—as he flipped us over.

He brushed his lips over the top of my head. "Don't go. Stay with me."

"I'm not going anywhere." I regretted the words as soon as they left my mouth.

It wasn't a lie, but what kind of future could we have together? I had responsibilities in a nether region while Monte's world was with the living. Not exactly a perfect match.

"Who called this morning?" he demanded.

That man would be the end of me, but maybe, just maybe, he'd help me figure a way out of my predicament. Would telling him the truth really hurt anything?

"I told you it was my roommate. When you arrived, I was on the phone with Hope."

"And?"

I sat up and moved away from Monte. Telling him might not hurt, but I couldn't look him in the eye and do it. "She had news for me."

"About your boss?"

"Yes. I expected Izanami would search for me. It's her job to know where death spirits are at all times, but Death is hunting for me too."

The mattress rocked as Monte came close. "Why?"

I swallowed hard. "Before I came to Havenwood Falls, Death let me know that I was to marry him. Turns out Izanami made a match between us."

"The fuck that's happening!" Monte exclaimed, leaping off the bed and picking up his jeans.

"Calm down." At that moment, a knock from Michaela would be welcome.

Monte's voice became as cold as ice and sharp like a scalpel. "Do you want the match?"

"No!" Slowly, I went over to him and ran my fingers over Monte's taut forearm. "We have to be smart about handling this. Nobody survives confrontations with entities like Death."

Monte nodded while his jaw clenched and unclenched.

"We need to deliver a message to Death. Preferably by someone who won't be afraid of the outcome."

Monte scrubbed a hand over his scruffy face. "There's a reaper in town. Maybe he'd do me a favor?"

"We won't know until we ask him."

CHAPTER 9

MONTE

*T*he last time I saw Shade was at the Dirty Knuckle. I shouldn't have assumed he'd still be in town or hanging out at the bar.

"You sure?" I asked, almost disbelieving that Shade simply vanished.

"Positive," Rhys said as he wiped down the counter. "He said something about work and then high-tailed it out of here."

Not the news we needed. Shade was the only direct line to Death that I knew.

Pandora glanced up at me. "Now what?"

I shrugged, not knowing the answer. Until the reaper returned, I hadn't a clue of how else to get information about the entity. "I'm sorry. I don't know what to tell you."

"I have a suggestion." Pandora took my hand. "We could find a hellhound. Their connection to Hell could be helpful."

Technically, I could go to Liam or Savage. They were hellhounds, but they had enough shit on their plates without me adding to it. There was another hellhound who'd help me out, though.

Oscar Vega, also known as Gunner, was the sergeant at arms for SIN.

At this time of day, if he wasn't at Cerberus Delivery handling business, he'd be at Get Buffed!.

The local gym was open to the general public, but from noon to two o'clock the facility closed down, and supernaturals were the only ones allowed inside. The one-story building was located on Petran near the clubhouse, making it convenient for any of the members to use. Lucky for us, the only vehicle in the lot was Oscar's bike.

A bell sounded as I pushed open the glass door. Pandora and I crossed the lobby. As we walked past the reception desk, we were met by the hulking hellhound.

I was at least an inch taller than Oscar, but he had me beat when it came to girth. The male had a frame like a Mack truck on steroids. The tank top and pants he wore looked like they were etched onto him. I guessed it added to the intimidating appearance.

Oscar pushed his shades into place as he dipped his chin. "Axel, didn't 'spect to see you here. Finally, thinkin' 'bout doing some trainin'?"

Lifting weights was never my idea of exercise. A good run through the mountains was enough to keep me fit. "Naw. Gotta few questions for you."

Oscar's gaze turned to Pandora, but his next words were meant for me. "When did you start hanging with reapers?"

She cleared her throat, put her hands on her curvy hips, and stared up at the hellhound. "I'm not a reaper, but I'd expect that assumption from the likes of you."

My heart stopped. Common sense dictated that you didn't insult someone you wanted a favor from. To my surprise, Oscar laughed loudly.

"I like this one, Axel. You should keep her around. " The hellhound folded his beefy arms over his broad chest. "What can I do for you, Miss Not-A-Reaper?"

Pandora grinned. "Death wants a wife, and I've been chosen for the deed."

Oscar let out a low whistle. "That's some fucked-up shit. Axel, what the hell have you gotten yourself into?"

I opened my mouth to speak, but Pandora held up her hand. "It's not Monte's fault. The arrangement was made by my employer, Madame Death, without my knowledge."

Oscar stroked his chin and cocked his head to one side. "So you're one of those fucking death spirits?" He shook his head, turned, and walked farther into the gym.

We followed behind, stopping in an area with treadmills and bikes. Oscar parked his ass on a piece of equipment that didn't look strong enough to hold him.

He glanced over his shoulder, as if we weren't actually alone, before continuing, "To be honest, hellhounds have nothing to do with the Japanese shadow realm Never even been to it. So what do you want from me?"

Pandora sighed. "I need to find out where Death is. He's coming after me."

Oscar and I both stared at her.

She pushed a hand through her long locks. "I left Yomi without Madame's permission."

"Wouldn't *she* be the one coming for you?" Oscar asked.

Pandora shook her head. "She won't leave the Land of the Dead. Instead, she'll dispatch her league of demon soldiers." Pandora regarded me with her bright green eyes. "I don't plan on returning to the shadow realm It's possible for me to stay a step ahead of the demons, but Death might be more of a challenge."

I didn't doubt for a minute that the entity would come to town searching for whatever—or whoever—he wanted.

Oscar scowled. "I really don't think I can help you. What you need is a bona fide reaper. But—"

"You'll keep your ear tuned?" she urged. "If you hear anything, will you let Monte know?"

Slowly, Oscar's lips turned up—a rarity for the hellhound. "I can do that."

I stepped forward and extended my hand to my brother in crime. "Thanks, man."

Not letting up on his grip, Oscar pulled me in. "Do whatever is needed to keep that one. You seem happy with her."

After settling things with Oscar, I played tour guide. While checking out the shops in the town square, Pandora noticed Callie's Consignments.

"Can we, Monte? I've never been inside a real store."

A response wasn't necessary. She practically dragged me into the consignment shop. Callie, a gypsy demon and the shop's owner, looked up as we entered.

"Be with you in a minute," she called out, and went back to ringing up a customer.

I really didn't expect to see her here, since she'd been traveling with Ronan. Her cousin, Nikita, had been managing the shop in her absence.

Pandora walked ahead of me, touching every rack as she moved. I chuckled softly. Watching her was like watching a kid in a toy store. Slowly, it sunk in that there were things in the world she had yet to experience.

By the time we reached the center of the room, the olive-skinned woman with waist-length brown hair had stepped from behind the counter. She smiled at us and said, "Apparently, Hunter James started a SIN shopping frenzy. I've never seen so many biker dudes wanting to touch vintage clothing in my life."

"Yeah, my friend doesn't mind shopping where I—"

"Can't stand it," Callie chimed in. She looked at Pandora. "So this visit is *your* idea?"

"Guilty." She extended her hand. "The name's Pandora."

"Callie. What can I help you find?"

"A pair of jeans. I've never worn them," Pandora admitted.

Callie's forehead furrowed. "Follow me. I just got in a few new pairs, mostly designer. I'm sure we'll find something you'll like."

While the ladies headed to the back, I did my own perusal of the racks. One never knew what they'd find in Callie's. Hunter picked up Izzie's engagement ring from there. Izzie even found her wedding dress in the shop. Me? I was just killing some time. It wasn't like I was in the market for anything special.

Not yet, but one of these days . . .

"What do you think?" Callie's voice floated toward me.

Turning around, I saw a breathtaking vision of loveliness. Pandora spun around, wearing a pair of curve-hugging jeans with a V-neck sweater that matched her jade-green eyes. I didn't know which look I preferred—that one or the black leather. Either way, she was stunning.

"It's perfect," I said.

"You think so?" Pandora asked. "This is so casual, but I like it."

Callie held up a brown suede jacket. "You might want this. It's getting a little nippy outside."

Pandora slipped it on and sank her hands in the pockets. "This feels nice. I'll take it."

"Go ahead and ring it all up." I removed my wallet.

"No, Monte," Pandora protested. "I do have money."

"How?"

She lowered her voice and explained, "It's a necessity when escorts enter this world."

"Understood, but let me do this. It's a gift."

Her eyebrows touched before she bent her head, allowing me to settle the bill.

Callie placed Pandora's clothes in a bag. Leaning over the counter, she lowered her voice and said, "It's good to see you with someone. It's been a long time, Montezuma."

"Yeah, it has." I glimpsed over at the female who made my pulse quicken. "Too long."

We thanked Callie for her help and headed out. The sun was beginning to set, and my stomach growled, affirming it was getting late.

"Hungry?" I asked.

Pandora slid her hand around my elbow. "I could eat."

"Good. I know just the place."

In a matter of minutes, I parked my truck in the parking lot for Burger Bar. In all honesty, I probably ate there at least once a week. Something about a well-cooked burger and a chocolate shake just made everything all right.

Pandora bit down on her burger, and her eyes rolled. She grabbed a napkin and wiped the mayo from her mouth. "This is so good! We have nothing like this in my world."

I pushed a basket of fries toward her. "Don't forget these. They're to die for."

Her eyebrows lifted as she looked at me.

Poor choice of words. "It just means that they're really good."

"Oh." She dabbed at her mouth again. "Thanks for this."

"For what?"

"Showing me your town, buying the clothes, this meal . . . It was very nice of you."

There was something about Pandora's tone that sounded foreboding, as if she still planned to leave. I was being stupid. Of course, she couldn't stay in Havenwood Falls, and I couldn't live in her world. We both knew it. I just wanted to ignore the facts for as long as I could.

Forcing a smile, I said, "It was nothing. If anything, I should be thanking you."

"And why is that?" She dropped the napkin on the table.

"You pulled me out of my routine—something I desperately needed."

Pandora reached for my hand. "You demanded honesty from me. Isn't it time you did the same?"

The moment I dreaded. "But not here. Let's head back to my place. What I have to say shouldn't be said in public."

We rode to my house in silence. I didn't know what was on Pandora's mind, but I was busy formulating how to explain my story. The last person I told it to . . . Well, she was no longer around.

Pandora removed her jacket, kicked off her shoes, and scooted into a corner of the sofa. "You don't have to tell me if you don't want to."

"No. I do." I shrugged out of my own jacket and sat beside her. "I told you some of this already."

"You said you came here with your grandparents when you were fourteen."

"Right. I just didn't tell you how serious it was." I leaned forward and rested my elbows on my knees. It was harder than I thought it would be.

Pandora touched my back. "You mentioned being in trouble with the government and something about computers."

"My cousin used to dare me to hack into mainframes. One night, he asked me to crack into a server." I side-glanced at Pandora. "He gave me the details, but I didn't know it belonged to the FBI. Next thing I knew, the cops were at my parents' door."

"Surely they didn't believe you did it?"

"I've always been tall for my age . . . Mom and Dad got a lawyer who said I was looking at a stint in juvie."

"Juvie?"

"Prison for youth offenders." I paused for a moment. "I was fortunate that my grandparents were in town. They offered to take me with them. I had no idea they lived in Havenwood Falls."

"But that doesn't explain why you spend so much time alone."

"I'm getting there." I shoved to my feet and paced the floor. "Three years ago, I had a girlfriend. Lianne was the—"

"Monte?"

I stopped moving. "Yeah?"

"The details aren't necessary. Just tell me what happened to her."

"She died. Fucking freak accident. Lianne went on a trip outside of Havenwood Falls. Sheriff Kasun said the vehicle wrecked shortly after leaving town. No explanation of how it happened."

Suddenly, Pandora's hands went around my waist. She placed her head on my chest. "I get it."

I wrapped my arms around the female. "It took me months to get over Lianne's death. My grandparents told me it wasn't my fault, but they didn't know the truth."

"Which was?"

"We had a damned fight before she left. Lianne didn't want me in SIN. She said they'd only use me."

"Lianne knew about the hacking?"

"Yeah, but I thought she was trying to fucking control me. The next day, she came by the apartment. Told me she was leaving town for a few days. I told her that if she left, I didn't want to see her again."

Pandora rubbed my back. "Why did you lie?"

"That's who I was then. Lying seemed easier than the truth. There was a lot of shit about me that Lianne didn't know, including me being a nagual. Despite her wishes, I joined SIN along with Hunter. He convinced me that I needed them in my life."

"I'm sorry about Lianne."

"Don't be." I didn't deserve Pandora's sympathy. "After the funeral, I threw myself into the club. Became the best damned prospect SIN ever had. If I wasn't at the clubhouse, I was at work. Staying busy kept me from getting involved with someone else," I admitted.

"Oh, my poor, misguided soul." Pandora gazed up at me. "What happened to Lianne wasn't your fault. Most likely, it was how she was meant to go. Punishing yourself isn't absolution. Havenwood Falls is supposed to be a haven, not a prison."

I gave her a wry smile. "I know that now."

"Good. Can we sit down? Because I really want to kiss you."

CHAPTER 10

PANDORA

I was on my knees writhing in ecstasy while Monte rode my body like a beast. The slap of flesh on flesh filled the room while loud moans from the both of us created a sensual, underlying rhythm. His pulsing cock, moving hard and fast, jackhammered toward a desperate climax. Monte clasped my hips, pulled me hard into his final thrust, and he came with an earthshaking cry. Seconds later, his rough motion sent me over the edge. As always, it was wave upon wave of luxurious sensations. We remained in the awkward position—Monte resting against my back—for a few minutes as our bodies recovered.

Monte made it overwhelmingly difficult not to fall for him. It was more than his handsome face, flawless physique, and undeniable chemistry. For me, it was the possibility of a simple lifestyle—free from concerns and the chaos that sometimes accompanied death. He was a man who would be so easy to love. *If* I had permission to do so.

The shifter wasn't the pretentious type. I'd had my fill of that kind of man during my existence. Men whose entire lives were predicated on appearance. Men who spent their days chasing down frivolous pursuits. It wasn't until death stared them in the face that they even tried to embrace anything significant. But that wasn't the case with Monte. He was as real as real could get. And underneath his laid-back exterior was a heart of gold—a rarity in the human world. Probably even more rare amongst supes. Great traits if I were looking for someone to love, but that couldn't happen—wouldn't happen—for a death spirit.

Or could it?

Lying beside Monte, I snuggled closer to him and thought about it some more. Entities fell in love quite frequently. Some of the greatest fictionalized romances had a basis in the passion between gods and goddesses. For the first time, I considered why shinigami had to be so different.

"Perhaps we're looking at the situation all wrong," I said out loud.

Monte intertwined his fingers with mine and squeezed. "Oh, I think I see this one quite clearly."

So did I, but his stiffening dick wasn't the one I referred to. I pulled the blanket over us. "Not that one, silly. I'm talking about my predicament with Death."

"Do tell." Monte lifted our joined hands and kissed the back of mine.

"Ever since Izanami pulled me out of the ether and gave me life, I'd been told that shinigami don't fall in love. We can't—"

Monte pushed up on his elbows and looked down at me. "Why not? Who made that rule?"

Shrugging, I said, "I'm guessing it was Izanami. After all, she was the one who said that emotions interfered with our purpose."

He dragged a hand through his hair. "She told you that? Is it documented somewhere? I understand that the Japanese underworld—"

"Yomi," I corrected. "The Japanese underworld could also apply to the yakuza—the human mafia." Madame Death was nefarious, but I'd rather deal with her than the legendary crime syndicate. Her agony lasted but a moment while theirs could be endless for the victims they tortured.

"I understand that Yomi is different from Hell, but something doesn't sound right about her explanation." Monte's brow furrowed deeply. "Remember the reaper I was looking for?"

"The one we sought at the bar? He left on a job, right?"

"He came to Havenwood Falls because of work and managed to fall in love while he was here." Monte slipped out of bed and put on his jeans.

"Your point?"

"If one of Death's reapers can love, why can't you? On top of that, have you thought any more about the agreement?"

"You mean the marriage to Death." The idea sent a feverish chill down my spine. I rubbed my upper arms. "I haven't been able to stop thinking of it."

"He wants a wife, which means he can feel. It also means that you are more than just an empty vessel escorting human souls to their final resting place." Monte faced me. "I think your creator lied to you."

My mouth fell open.

"Why would she do that to you?" Monte tugged on his T-shirt and then sat on the edge of the bed. "Want to hear my answer?"

I nodded, unable to find the words.

"If this pact with Death was made after your creation, then she had to tell you that nonsense. Otherwise, you would have found someone, and the agreement would have been threatened."

"But my roommate . . . All shinigami . . ." I stopped myself. Hope was the only other spirit that believed Madame Death's rhetoric. I'd never heard anyone else mention it. My time in Havenwood Falls, along with Addie's tattoo, must have altered my makeup. I felt a horrid foreboding settle deep in my gut.

Monte touched my arm and grabbed my attention. "Call your roommate while I'm gone. Maybe she can fill in some details for you."

I squinted up at him. "Where are you going?"

"I've got church tonight."

"Church?" I tilted my head to the side. "I didn't take you for the religious type."

"Not that kind. It's what the club calls our meetings." He leaned in and brushed my lips with his. "I promise not to be long."

"Can I come?"

He touched my cheek. "Not even old ladies get to attend church."

"I am not *that* old!" A couple of centuries was approximately twenty human years in my world. Shinigami aged very slowly.

Monte chuckled. "That's not what it means. An old lady is a steady girlfriend. She supports her man, allowing him to fulfill his role with the club. Think of her as an asset—his right arm—so to speak."

Smiling, I asked, "Does that make me your old lady?"

"Only if you want that title. Personally, you're much more to me. All this time I've lived in darkness. You're the light showing me the right path." He kissed me again before grabbing his jacket and leaving.

Monte had it wrong. I was the one who had existed in the shadows. He gave form to the murkiness and provided much-needed clarity.

～

"Oh, I'm so glad you contacted me," Hope said. "Madame is furious."

"She has no right to be," I announced. "Not after what she's done."

Wariness seeped into my partner's voice. "What's happened, Pandora?"

Ignoring her question for a moment, I said, "You know Toshi?"

"The handsy spirit? What about him?"

"That male doesn't hesitate to put the moves on us. But what does Madame constantly say about entanglements?"

"That we're not supposed to date our own. We're not to have sex with our own. We can't . . ." Panic entered her tone. "Pandora, what have you done?"

"Nothing. Izanami's been feeding us a serious load of bullshit. Why is it okay for Toshi to keep pursuing us? I've even seen him with other females. If it's forbidden for *us* to get involved with our own kind, why are *they* allowed to break the rule?"

The phone went silent.

"Hope?"

"I'm still here. Just trying to wrap my head around what you're saying. Why would Izanami lie to us?"

"Control—pure and simple." It was the only explanation I had. "Do me a favor and speak to Toshi. Find out what he's been told about relationships."

"Want me to have him call you?"

"No!" The last thing I needed was for him to locate me. Toshi was as sly as a kitsune. For all I knew, he'd use the info for his own gain. "I'll call you again tomorrow."

"Pandora, can I ask you about your dream man?"

It took her long enough to get around to it. "He wasn't just a dream. He's real and a good man."

"You do remember your engagement to Death?"

"I'd like to forget it, but I can't. To be honest, Madame's lies should make the arrangement null and void."

"It should, but . . . I hear that Death is very forgiving."

"Let's pray that the rumors aren't wrong."

Unable to sit still and let life unfold, I returned to the inn. Thankfully, the person I wanted to speak with was in the lobby with Michaela. Both ladies looked up as I crossed the floor.

"Hello, stranger," Addie said. "Enjoying your stay?"

I cut my gaze toward Michaela who smiled broadly. "What did you tell her?"

"Nothing that nobody couldn't see for themselves." The moroi vampire laughed. "Hate to tell you, but everyone in town knows about you spending time with Monte."

My cheeks heated.

"Don't be embarrassed," Addie said. "Everyone is so happy that Monte's getting out again."

Recalling the conversation I had earlier with him, I asked, "Was it really that bad?" When the two friends exchanged a knowing look, I added, "He told me about Lianne."

Addie sighed. "It was. After her death, Monte sealed himself off from everyone. Thank goodness for Hunter James. He talked some sense into Monte and together they prospected SIN."

"That's his best friend, right?"

"Yes. But what happened with Lianne was before I came back," Michaela said.

Addie nodded.

"If Lianne was upset about Monte joining the club, why would he go through with it?"

Addie took a sip from a ceramic mug. "Hunter encouraged it. I guess he saw it as a way for Monte to move past Lianne's death."

"A distraction," I said, understanding. If it hadn't been for the motorcycle club, Monte probably would have become a hermit.

"Exactly," the women said in unison.

"Something tells me that's not why you were looking for me," Addie said.

"It wasn't. Is there somewhere—"

Michaela smiled. "The library is empty, if you want to use it."

Addie and I entered a room with floor-to-ceiling bookcases lining all the walls but one. The small space included comfy-looking arm chairs. We sat down in front of the only window in the room affording a view of the town square. The idyllic scene didn't hint at the supernaturals living in Havenwood Falls—just peace.

"What's up, Pandora?"

"I've got a bit of a problem." I fiddled with my jacket's zipper.

"With Death or your employer?"

My eyes widened.

"Don't be surprised. Michaela was at the Dirty Knuckle earlier and overheard Oscar Vega talking about your situation. He was looking for Shade." Before I could speak, Addie said, "Michaela only mentioned it because she was concerned. She was going to say something about it to you or Monte."

Slowly, my blood pressure rose. I didn't need the hellhound spreading my business around town, which forced me to ask, "How protected am I here?"

Addie leaned forward. "Normally, nobody can find us. But we've had some problems, prompting us to tighten the wards around the town."

I noticed how she seemed to sidestep my question, but I didn't want to call her out on it. Instead, I asked, "Do those wards keep out all forces?"

"No, but we have alarms. We'll know right away if Death or Izanami breeches the wards."

"What about other death spirits?"

"You're talking about deadly shinigami? Same thing. The best we can do is respond if they arrive." Addie studied me for a moment. "Do you really think your employer will come after you?"

"Not sure." It was an honest answer. "I contacted my roommate back in Yomi. She'll ask around and let me know what's going on."

Addie pursed her lips. "If you learn anything that I should know, please—"

"I will." I didn't want to become a burden or do anything to destroy the semblance of tranquility in town.

She smiled. "By the way, how are things going with Monte?"

"Very well."

The girl pushed up her glasses as she studied me. "But you're worried about the relationship."

"No, I'm not. I'm concerned about the risk."

"Tell me about it."

So I shared my worst fears with her.

CHAPTER 11

MONTE

Although I told Pandora there was nothing religious about SIN's church, it was our once-a-week personal come-to-Jesus moment. In that forum, the minister was an intimidating hellhound who had a generous side not known to everyone.

Liam Peters was as blunt as a motherfucker and as demanding as the Devil himself might be, but I loved him like he was blood. I'd lay down my life for him—for any of those guys—any damned day of the week.

After we discussed business—mostly details about some dispatch changes regarding Cerberus Delivery—I pulled Liam to the side. "Got a minute?"

He stroked the stubble on his jaw. "Sure. Whatcha need?"

"In private?"

Despite the dark glasses, I felt the hellhound's surprised stare right before he cleared his throat. "Yo, get the hell out! I need the goddamned room."

Chairs scraped, and heavy feet shuffled across the floor amid disgruntled voices as the men emptied from the space. Hunter frowned as he glanced back at me.

"Don't worry, man. I'll call you." Hopefully, I conveyed the right sentiment. I didn't want my friend overly concerned.

Hunter's eyebrows shot up. His gaze traveled between Liam and me, then he dipped his chin before leaving with the rest of the members.

Savage was the last to walk out. With a hand on the doorknob, he stopped and said, "You need me?"

Realizing that his input might be a good idea, I nodded.

He pushed the door shut and plopped his large frame down into a seat. "What the fuck is going on, Axel?"

"I met someone."

No matter how long I hung out with these men, I'd always be a little nervous when asking them for favors. Just like my actual siblings, whom I hadn't seen in years, I looked up to them. Hell, I idolized them, especially those two. Shit didn't stop them. When either man wanted something, he claimed it—property or women. It didn't matter to them.

Before Liam uttered a word, Savage jumped in. "This meeting is about a woman?" He waggled his bushy eyebrows and let out a low whistle. "Somebody's finally getting some ass."

The ghost of a smile crossed Liam's face. "So what's the damned problem?"

I exhaled loudly. "She's a Japanese death spirit, and Death wants her for his wife."

Savage snorted. "That pencil-dick fucker wouldn't know the first thing to do with one."

Liam looked at his friend as he rubbed a hand over his jaw. He adjusted his shades and said, "First, you need to stop telling shit to Gunner. That fucker told me about this shit before tonight's church."

Duly noted. I'd heard rumors that Oscar was worse than a female, but I was never one to believe random gossip. In the future, I needed to do a better job at listening to the idle chit-chat that surfaced apart from the darknet.

"Second," started Savage, "what the hell do you think we can do? We don't work for Death."

"But there are some demons that know him," Liam pointed out.

"Maybe," Savage agreed. "Think they'd help?"

Liam scowled. "Couldn't hurt to find out."

My gaze bounced from one end of the table to the other. The back and forth between the two hellhounds gave me a headache. I had the profound feeling that discussing my business—Pandora's business—with them was a huge mistake. Unfortunately, I couldn't take shit back.

"If I were you," Liam said, "I'd be pissed as fuck."

"Yeah, I am." Keeping my gaze down, I laid my hand flat on the table and traced the inlaid wooden pattern with my fingers. Glancing up, I said, "I want a goddamned meeting with Death."

Savage and Liam exchanged a look right before they burst out laughing.

"You're kidding, right?" said Savage, wiping at his eyes. "Nobody has a meeting with fucking Death and lives to talk about it."

Liam did a better job at regaining his composure. When our eyes met, he cleared his throat while Savage fought back his laughter.

Pirate said, "Listen, you're our brother, Axel. We want nothing but your happiness, so I tell you what we're gonna do. We'll ask around. See if there's any way to get word to Death. If it can be done and he agrees, you'll meet with him here. Understood?"

"Yeah."

"But tell me this. What do you plan on doing if the asshole won't give up on your lady? We got enough shit going on in town. We don't need the Court coming down on us 'bout this situation." Liam paused for a beat, letting the words sink in.

Savage concurred with a grunt.

"We can't afford any missteps, Monte. Trust me—if we create havoc, the Court will chew our asses up and possibly kick out the MC," Liam said. "Ain't happening. Got it?"

Honestly, I hadn't thought hard enough about my demand, but there was one thing I was sure of. When it came to Pandora, I'd stand up for her—no matter what. She was important to me.

"I'm prepared to do whatever it takes," I affirmed.

Savage snorted again. "Aw, man. We'd better take your goddamned measurements while you're here. Get that pine box ready."

Despite his demeanor, I knew the hellhound only had my best interests at heart. They both did. Hopefully, nobody was going out in a damned box. I had a lot of living to make up for. Dying didn't fit into the equation.

I pushed to my feet, bobbed my head, and walked to the exit with the sound of Savage and Liam's conversation following me down the hall.

Night had fallen by the time I stepped into the parking lot. I pulled my jacket closed and looked up into the dark sky before glancing over at my bike. As expected, Hunter waited for me. I shook my head and strolled over to him with a smile on my face.

"I thought I said I'd call you."

"You know me." He grinned. "I don't wait for shit." Hunter lightly punched my arm. "What's going on, man?"

"You in a hurry to get home?" Truthfully, I wanted to get back to Pandora, but wrapping up that business took precedence over my desire.

"Naw. Izzie's working late tonight. Let's head over to the Haven."

The Haven Saloon, owned by Bent Brent, was the only place in town where you could get drunk and high at the same time, thanks to him smoking weed behind the counter. We entered the bar, and Brent—surrounded by thick smoke—waved to us as he lifted a joint to his lips. For a moment, I wondered how many brain cells he destroyed on a daily basis.

Hunter and I grabbed a corner booth. Within minutes, Brent ambled over to us with a couple of beers. "The usual, right?"

Grateful to be a creature of habit, I reached for the frosty bottle. "Thanks, Brent."

As soon as he walked away, Hunter asked, "So what happened after I left?"

"Asked Liam and Savage for a favor." I turned up the beer and stared at my friend.

"No shit?" He took a deep swig. "Anything to do with the female you've been keeping time with?"

"Yeah," I said, lowering the bottle. "Pandora's in a bad situation with Death."

Hunter's eyes bulged. "The head reaper?"

"Yeah. I asked Liam to set up a meeting with him."

Hunter spat out his beer. "What the fuck? Have you lost your damned mind?"

"Not hardly, but I'm not ready to give up Pandora just because a couple of beings with splinters shoved up their asses are using her like a game piece."

Hunter coughed, still trying to clear his voice, but it came out husky. "Okay. When is this meeting? I'm going with you."

"It's not like you—"

His green eyes darkened. "I'm not letting you do this alone. We're brothers. We've been through a lot of shit together, and I'm not bowing out now."

Truth be told, if it weren't for Hunter, I would have never survived Lianne's death. Before that tragic event, he helped me find myself in a town full of strangers. Without Hunter in my life, I'd probably be a fucking geek working a nine to five. Deep down, I was glad for his support.

"Okay, we'll do it together, but I have to wait on Liam. He's going to ask around and try to set something up."

My friend's mouth opened and closed but nothing came forth. Instead, he shook his head and returned to his drink.

"You think I'm crazy?" I pulled at the gold label on the bottle. Honestly, if Hunter wasn't questioning my sanity, I was. No sane person volunteered to meet with Death.

"Not exactly the word I'd use." He took another pull from the bottle, then said, "This woman makes you happy."

It wasn't a question. Just a statement of fact. Something I wouldn't deny.

"Monte, if she's really important to you, then you need to do whatever it takes to hang onto her. You can't afford to go fucking backward. Know what I mean?"

I nodded, but my friend had more to say.

"Before Pandora, you were as predictable as a fucking clock. Now, nobody knows what you're doing or when you'll show up." He glanced at me with a crooked grin. "Don't get me wrong. That's a good thing. Only fuckers without lives are that reliable."

A nervous flutter hit my gut. "What are you saying?"

"Only that you deserve Pandora, even if I don't approve of what you're willing to do for her."

"Thank you."

"Don't thank me yet. You're in for a serious battle. I don't know what I'll do if you lose."

"That makes two of us."

Hunter's words stayed with me on the ride home. Getting into an altercation with a supreme entity wasn't the wisest thing I'd ever done. After hacking into the FBI's computers, I swore I'd make better choices. Lianne's death made keeping that vow possible. But with Pandora . . . I guess when it came to matters of the heart, wisdom took a back seat.

CHAPTER 12

PANDORA

*A*fter spilling all that I knew to Addie, she seemed to be at a loss for words, like she didn't believe me, but I hadn't lied about the risk. At any minute, Death could enter Havenwood Falls and claim me. Provided Izanami didn't break her own vow never to leave Yomi. I could very well hasten a supernatural apocalypse in the quaint town.

"Maybe Death can be reasoned with? You know, maybe if your employer sees that you're happy . . ." Addie's voice trailed off.

Was she kidding? Reason with Death and Izanami? "Have you ever dealt with an immortal entity?"

Addie lifted an eyebrow.

Unsure whether I'd offended her, I blurted out, "I'm sorry. I assumed you—"

She lifted her palm. "It's nothing I'm at liberty to discuss. Just trust me when I say that I'm experienced in that department."

I held my tongue. News of the Collector had reached the shadow realm. The details of that event were sketchy, and it wasn't my place to ask about them. Besides, it was best not to divulge what I knew to Addie. The supes in Havenwood Falls probably thought no one else knew what had happened. Sadly, entities in high and low places were well aware of the Collector.

Addie pushed to her feet. "I'm trusting that it will all work out, but should there be any problems . . ."

I didn't share her optimism. "I'll be sure to reach out to you. Thanks for listening."

"Any time."

I watched her leave before making my own exit. Instead of returning to Monte's house, I went up to my room, determined to get some answers for myself. Toshi, the death spirit dying to get into my panties, picked up on the first ring.

"I was wondering how long it would take you to call, Takara," he uttered.

A hint of sensuousness slipped into his voice, and I had to choke back the bile. "You know I go by Pandora. Please refrain from—"

He laughed heartily.

"I fail to see what's so damned funny." Did I mention how much I disliked him?

"Takara-chan, you're far too serious. I suspect that's why you're in a world of trouble."

Kicking off my shoes, I plopped down on the bed. I hated how Toshi took the liberty of using my given name, but to use it affectionately was even worse. I had a choice—get the information I needed or dwell on how he referred to me.

"What do you know?"

"That our boss is very disappointed with you. And Death is beyond upset. He expected to be married to you by now."

Not news. I needed more. "Never mind that, Toshi. What did Izanami tell you about shinigami?"

"Be specific, Takara-chan. Our boss has told me many, many things."

I tapped my fingers against my thigh as the words rushed from my mouth. "Our rules, Toshi. What do you know about them?"

"They're different, depending on what group you belong to. The escorts who were created on the day you were formed must remain pure outside of their assignments."

Pure? Perhaps that was what Madame Death meant when she said that emotions distracted us.

My neck stiffened. "What about those not created with me? What rules do they follow?"

"We're free to do whatever we please as long as we remain loyal to Madame. Remember, I'm not an escort."

"I don't follow," I admitted.

"Very well, Takara-chan, I shall educate you."

Toshi, a traditional spirit who had retired from active duty, spent the next minutes explaining to me that Madame created shinigami in clusters. Most were made to fulfill the traditional purpose—*inviting* humans to death. They were scary spirits who claimed lives on a daily basis. The escorts were meant to gently guide souls. But it was all an experiment. Madame was pitting the two classes against each other. If escorts did a better—more efficient—job of guiding humans to the afterlife, she'd cease creating the traditional shinigami. It was why the latter type worked harder and harder these days.

Hearing the truth behind my existence angered me. I held my phone tightly until I heard a slight crack and then eased up on my grip. "What about the pact between Izanami and Death?"

There was a great chance that Madame didn't share everything with a lowly assistant.

"Ahhh . . . that . . ." I thought Toshi wasn't going to tell me what he knew, but then he said, "Every hundred years, she creates the perfect escort."

"Perfect how?" I folded my legs beneath me.

"An escort that would appeal to Death. One formed with a heart but no soul."

Good thing I wasn't standing. My vision blurred as I drew in a deep breath. Panic swelled inside of me as my breath snagged on something within my chest. I couldn't speak.

"Takara? Are you still there?"

"Yes, I'm here." I pushed down the growing anxiety. "Wouldn't this escort know if he or she had a heart?"

"Under everyday circumstances? No."

He meant while in service. As long as that escort did his or her duties as instructed, nothing unusual would be noticed.

"Takara-chan, I think you already know the answer you seek. I know for a fact that you discovered your heart years ago with the dream."

The anxiety became a ball in my gut. "How?"

"It's why Izanami was so upset. The more you mentioned it, the angrier she became. I walked in on her one day during a rant. She let it slip that you were never supposed to have that dream. It irked her that some goddess—or god—intervened in her plans."

A deity intervened on my behalf?

Toshi's revelation didn't sit well with me, but I had to know more. "Tell me about my heart."

"I can't tell you what you want to know. I can tell you that the closer you came to discovering the man from your dream, the stronger your heartbeat grew. It's why you left Yomi. I realized the truth as soon as I heard you were gone. Madame knows too."

It explained why she wanted me to ignore my dream. She didn't want me to learn any of what Toshi said. "Was I supposed to find out these things?"

"Your heart would have been revealed when you met the one meant for you. Despite the arrangement, Death isn't the one for you."

"Stop speaking in riddles!"

"I'm surprised you don't know this. Death was there on the day of your creation. He told Izanami she had failed to fulfill their bargain and demanded that the next shinigami pulled from the ether would belong to him."

"Me."

"Give the death spirit her prize," Toshi said smugly before he paused for a moment. "Takara-chan, you should return to Yomi. Apologize to Izanami, and then take your place beside Death."

"No," I protested. "You said he wasn't meant—"

Toshi chuckled. "What I say does not matter. We all exist according to Izanami's dictates. If you don't honor the pact, someone else will be chosen. Madame will return you to the shadows."

Thank you, but no thanks. "I'll take my chances."

"Suit yourself."

After disconnecting, I tossed my phone on the bed and lay back, trying to wrap my head around Toshi's words. Death and Izanami had no business creating death spirits for their own twisted purposes. Since they didn't serve the same world, I didn't understand their motivation. Death overstepped his boundaries by crossing over into the shadow realm. Why couldn't he choose a paramour from the many souls who were escorted into the afterlife? Why me?

Suddenly, my phone buzzed with a text message.

Death: Hello, Takara. I wanted you to know that I'll be in

Havenwood Falls midnight tomorrow. I've been exceedingly patient with you, but I will wait no more. I will not leave without you by my side.

I stared at the screen, wondering if I should reply. Honestly, what would be the point? If anything, he might show up sooner. Instead, I tucked the phone into my pocket and put on my shoes. There was someplace else I desperately needed to be.

It was a crisp night, but the breeze was refreshing. I pulled up the collar on my jacket and sank my hands into my pockets as I sat on Monte's front steps. It was the first time that I really noticed the chill, but my mind was too occupied to care.

I had a heart.

That was why I always felt a strange tug when I got to know my marks. Hope often teased that I was overthinking my job.

I had a heart.

It was the reason why I sometimes felt sadness after an assignment. Unlike other death spirits, I lingered between realms and watched a departing soul. Because . . .

I had a heart.

Its presence clarified the chemistry between Monte and me. It was more than a physical attraction. When we first kissed, I felt the spark —like I'd found something I didn't know was lost.

I. Had. A. Heart.

And it beat for *him*.

Having a heart meant I had something else—something more relevant. It was a theory worth testing.

Monte wore a jade jaguar's head on a strip of leather around his neck. I assumed it represented his inner beast. He never explained what else it symbolized, but I had an idea. Closing my eyes, I held out my palm and imagined a similar piece of jewelry in the form of a skull. I wrapped my hand around the pendant briefly before slipping it into my pocket. Deep down, I suspected that Toshi may have lied about one thing. If he did, I'd soon have proof.

"Hey," Monte said, snagging my attention.

I glanced up and sashayed over to him. "Hey, yourself. How was church?"

"The usual BS." He gave me a quick kiss, grabbed my hand, and led me inside. "You and I have to talk."

As soon as we entered the house, I said, "I have something important to tell—"

Monte covered my mouth with a finger. "Let me go first. After I finish what I have to say, you might choose to leave me behind."

My stomach fluttered. What on earth could Monte say that would make me walk away from him? I fought back the nerves and sat down, but my eyes stayed on the jade pendant around Monte's neck. "Go ahead."

"After church I spoke with the prez. Liam's a hellhound with connections. I asked him to set up a meeting with Death."

My newly discovered heart thumped painfully in my chest. I swallowed hard. "You got your meeting."

Monte's eyebrows knitted together. "Huh?"

"I got a text from Death. He let me know he's coming to town tomorrow. The meeting's at midnight."

Monte looked at me incredulously. "Death uses a cell phone?"

"Yeah. He's even on Instagram." It was my poor attempt at adding a little levity to the conversation. "He uses hashtag death on all of his posts. If it's creepy as all get out, it's his doing."

"You're serious?"

"Dea—" I caught myself and dropped the inappropriate wording. "You can't meet with him. The message said he won't leave Havenwood Falls without me."

"Not happening."

"Monte, he'll annihilate you."

The man who stirred my heart knelt in front of me, took my hand in his, and said, "I'm not afraid of him. For the first time in my life, I'm a hundred percent about something. Something—" His free hand suddenly went to his throat. "What the hell?"

I saw what he felt, and my lips curled up. The pale green pendant came to life, turning a deep shade of pink, while the one I owned warmed my pocket. Toshi had lied. Or more accurately, Izanami had lied to him. A heart wasn't the only thing making me special.

Monte jumped to his feet and ran upstairs. I followed and found him in the bathroom, staring wide-eyed into the mirror. "This isn't possible. The only time this happens is when a soul mate is near."

"I figured as much." Carefully, I reached into my jacket and removed the pendant, its glow matching Monte's.

He whirled around and gazed down at my hand. "How?"

"You should probably get comfortable. I have a lot to tell you."

It took a moment to tell Monte everything I'd learned from Toshi. When I was done, Monte stood and walked over to the bedroom window. Glancing over his shoulder, he asked, "You're certain?"

I rose up off the bed and went to him. Taking his hand, I placed it on my chest. "Have you not felt my heart beating? The pendant is proof that I have a soul too. My uniqueness is why Death wants me. Imagine what he could do with a death spirit that has both."

Monte cocked his head to the side. "He could use your genetics and create his own death spirits. Fuck, he could take over Yomi."

"Exactly." It was the conclusion I reached while waiting for Monte to return home. "He'd put Izanami out of business. The entity would become a god reigning over a vast portion of the shadow realm."

I stumbled across one more thing while sitting on the steps. The real reason why Izanami created escorts. Death wanted the traditional shinigami. He could add them to his ranks of sentinels. Escorts, on the other hand, wouldn't serve his purpose. Izanami wanted to destroy conventional death spirits, keeping them out of Death's hands, which would change Yomi forever.

"We have to stop him. But how?" said Monte.

Best question ever.

CHAPTER 13

MONTE

*A*round midnight I slipped out of bed and went to the window. Not because I heard anything. It was the meeting with Death weighing heavily on my mind. My concern was with how Death found Pandora.

I sent Liam a quick message. He hadn't had any luck finding Death, and was surprised that the entity was coming to town. My first thought was the reaper, Shade, but he hadn't returned. Maybe his employer was using him to garner information. Frankly, I hoped I was wrong.

However things went with Death, I wasn't afraid. If having Pandora by my side meant risking my life, I'd do it. Truthfully, I'd do anything to keep Pandora with me.

When I looked into the mirror, I no longer saw a man still grieving over his first love. That male was replaced by a being who wanted to live his life fully with the female who made his heart beat stronger. Finding out that the gorgeous death spirit was my soul mate erased all doubt. I wasn't sure of a lot of things—why I fucked up as a kid, why my grandparents took pity on me, or why Hunter became my friend—but I was sure of how I felt about Pandora.

Her hands wrapped around my waist, and she placed her cheek against my bare back. Honestly, I didn't understand everything that was happening between us. My deep feelings for Pandora seemed too sudden. Wasn't it supposed to take time to care for someone—to love someone?

I wasn't just questioning my emotions though. Something had changed with her as well. The first time I touched Pandora, her pale flesh was cool. During her short stay, it had taken on a new radiance. A golden color defined her cheeks while a warmth took over her body. It was as if someone had pushed her into the sunlight, and her skin soaked up the rays.

"Can't sleep?" she asked.

"No. It's nothing for you to worry about. You should get some—"

"Uh-uh," she protested. "If you aren't sleeping, neither will I."

I turned around and lowered my head, claiming her lips. Even her taste had changed. Kissing Pandora was like imbibing pure ambrosia. I couldn't—wouldn't—give that up for anything in the world or beyond it. Death was about to fuck around with the wrong shifter.

Morning came sooner than I would have liked. My head was foggy from lack of sleep while my body was sore from the sweet agony Pandora put me through. I cracked open my eyes and rolled over. Instead of lying beside me, she stood in the doorway wearing lingerie that should be illegal—a black leather-and-lace one-piece number that showcased her ample boobs. Fishnet stockings covered her legs, and thankfully, she didn't forget the high heels.

"Like what you see?" she asked seductively.

While my head struggled for a suitable answer, my dick stood at attention. Who turned down a little early morning fuckery? I planned to give Hozier's song about the world's screaming and heaving state a whole new definition.

The mattress dipped as Pandora crawled over me. As she straddled my crotch, I couldn't help but ask, "You're not planning anything kinky?"

She winked, and a set of handcuffs appeared in her hands.

"I should warn you," I said nervously. "Last time I had an encounter with those, it didn't turn out good for me."

Ignoring my forewarning, Pandora snapped the restraints onto my wrists. "Obviously, she didn't know what to do with them."

An unbridled sigh escaped my lips, and my pelvis lifted beneath her, begging for some release.

She touched my chest. "I plan on fucking your gorgeous body as if it were our last time together."

"Bring it."

My fingers longed to touch Pandora while my mouth wanted to taste her, but she was the only one enjoying those luxuries. Or so I thought. My naughty mate repositioned herself until her sweet pussy hovered over my face. I lifted my head and eagerly explored her, getting lost in her sweet juices.

Pandora moaned deeply, shifted her position, then wrapped her lips around my stiff cock.

Fucking 69!

I would have screamed if my mouth wasn't happily drowning in her succulent taste. Honestly, I could have died right then with my tongue buried between her legs. Who needed to go to Heaven? I was already paying homage at its gates.

An hour later, I rubbed my reddened wrists. Pandora pushed my hand aside and kissed the irritated skin. "I'm so sorry."

"Don't be." The memory of her riding me like a fucking stallion as I strained against the handcuffs was still fresh in my mind. It was a level of sex I'd never experienced, and my twitching dick echoed its delight. "I enjoyed every minute of it. How's your ass?"

She giggled. "It still stings a little."

When Pandora finally released me, she pulled out a red leather paddle. I was a bit hesitant to use it, but she assured me it was all right. I had to admit her moaning and the sound of the instrument striking her bare ass enticed me. Maybe it was that same type of excitement that had Hunter seeking out his proclivities.

Honestly, I didn't want to stoop to that level of sexual depravity.

"Now I'm the one sorry."

"No need. I encouraged it." She rolled onto her stomach and kicked her leg out from under the sheet.

"Should I ask where those things came from?"

"Just a little something from my bag of tricks. I encounter plenty of humans who want to indulge in a fantasy before leaving this life."

"Oh." For some reason, I felt a twinge of jealousy.

Pandora touched my cheek. "Monte, I love being with you, but this isn't just about sex. I've never felt like this before, and I don't want to be with anyone else."

I smiled and pushed a strand of hair off her face. "Same here."

"Good." She dropped a kiss on my abs. "So how does this soul mate thing work?"

I shrugged. "I didn't think it was something I'd ever have, so I kind of ignored the stuff my parents and grandparents told me. I only know what Hunter has said."

"Which is?"

"Izzie and Hunter share thoughts. Sometimes they communicate without words. He said they can sense each other too. Hunter knows when Izzie's in trouble. He can sense her location whenever they're not together. Same with her."

"That sounds like some wacky supernatural GPS."

Stroking my hand over her hip, I said, "Something like that." Her eyes met mine. "Have you—"

"Experienced that? I think we just did. Confession time?" She paused for a moment. "Last night, I knew why you couldn't sleep, but I don't think being mates or having some sort of connection had anything to do with it. Anyone could read your concern from a mile away."

I nodded. She wasn't the only one who had a confession. When I came home last night, I knew she was there before I even pulled up. At the time, I thought it was more like a premonition or the manifestation of a desire—I wanted her there and by coincidence she was. I refused to see anything more in it. Once the ordeal with Death was done, I planned to sit down with either Baba or my grandfather and get some real information. Until then, I planned to enjoy every minute with Pandora.

She cleared her throat. "You think meeting Death will be a simple ordeal that can easily be wrapped up?"

Okay. Forget what I just said. That woman did read my thoughts. I'd better watch myself around her. Fool around and think the wrong thing and . . .

She smirked and dipped her chin as if she knew. "Monte, you have yet to think of anything that would make me doubt you. And as far as your future thoughts, don't stop. I like them." Pandora sat up and let the sheet fall from her perfect breasts. "Right now, though, you have a choice to make. Either continue talking about Death and grandparents or fuck me like you mean it."

Slipping my arms around her, I chose the latter. A much more enjoyable option.

～

Pandora and I spent the better part of the day in bed. It was like sex for the condemned—get as much as you can because you don't know when it might happen again. *If ever again.* By nightfall, I was fairly certain that in the morning I'd have a crotch burn from the wear and tear. That was, if we got to see the next day.

After a few unsuccessful attempts to shower together—Pandora had become a horny nymph—I eventually got myself cleaned up and dressed, and she met me at the bottom of the stairs. Hunter and Izzie had invited us over for dinner, and we were late.

Frankly, I was nervous. No one else had actually seen us together as a couple, but everyone in Havenwood Falls probably knew about Pandora and me. My biggest fear was that Izzie wouldn't accept Pandora. Thankfully, my concern turned out to be completely irrational. Izzie and my mate—would I ever get sick of saying that?— hit it off over a bottle of Shiraz.

"Come with me," Hunter said, and we left the females out on the deck.

Closing the patio door behind me, I asked, "Do you think it's okay to leave them alone?"

"Man, you're worrying for nothing. You know Izzie. If she had issues with Pandora, my wife would have said it by now." He opened the oven and pulled out a casserole dish.

"What's for dinner, anyway?"

"Baba made a lasagna." He rolled his eyes. "I asked him to make something else. He thought this was best."

"Doesn't matter," I said. "Whatever he makes is good."

"True that, brother." Hunter turned off the oven. "When do we meet up with Death?"

"About that—"

"No." He glared at me. "I told you I'm coming too. Izzie will stay here with Pandora. What time is it?"

Reluctantly, I said, "Midnight."

"At the clubhouse?"

I nodded.

"Okay." Hunter's gaze softened a bit. "Monte, I made a promise to you years ago. Remember it?"

"Yeah." It was a silly vow he made when we were kids, and I'd told him the truth about why I was in Havenwood Falls. "Come hell or high water, whether it be human or supernatural, you will always have my back. Now and right through eternity."

"I meant it then, and I mean it now. You don't do this shit without me."

I tried hard to enjoy the dinner. The food was good and so was the conversation, but I couldn't stop looking at my phone. Every now and then, Pandora would glance over at me with a look that said to stop worrying. At some point, I needed to learn how to shield my thoughts.

She glared at me, and I quickly dismissed that idea.

"What's this about you two being soul mates?" Izzie asked as she poured more wine.

Pandora smiled. "It's a recent development."

"Then we have a lot to talk about tonight while the guys are gone."

My mate's gaze whipped to me. "What is she talking about?"

Hunter stood and picked up his plate. "Izzie, why don't we gather up the dishes?"

Her mouth opened but quickly shut when Hunter shook his head. Izzie grabbed her plate and followed him out of the dining room.

"Pandora."

She glowered at me while pursing her lips. "You're not leaving me behind, Monte. You need me with you."

"It's safer—"

"No, it's not. If Death decides to kill you, I can bring you back. Without me, you're dead."

Not exactly the words I wanted to hear. Part of me wanted to argue the case for her staying away, but when Pandora cast those alluring green eyes at me and batted those long lashes, I gave in. "It's against my better judgment—"

Pandora got out of her seat and came over to me. Kissing my cheek, she said, "Do you trust me?"

"With my life."

"Then believe me when I say that I have to be at the meeting."

CHAPTER 14

MONTE

*R*iding toward the clubhouse with my mate's arms wrapped around my waist should have made me less nervous or at least provided a bit of distraction. Instead, Pandora's presence ratcheted up my anxiety several notches. So much so that I was a sweaty mess by the time I turned into the lot.

After Hunter and I parked our bikes, Pandora pulled me to the side. "Are you going to be all right?"

"I will," I lied.

"Don't," she said. "You're nervous. I wouldn't blame you if you didn't want to do this."

"Pandora, there's nothing I wouldn't do for you. Okay?"

She opened her mouth, but I quickly kissed her. When I dragged my mouth from hers, tears shone in her eyes.

"You asked me to trust you. Now I'm asking the same of you."

She gave me a sad look, and then we reluctantly followed Hunter inside. When I saw Liam and Savage, however, I froze in my tracks.

"What are you two doing here?"

Savage glared at me. "We were at Cerberus. Some shit went down . . ."

Liam held up his palm. "We were in the parking lot when the lights started flickering at the club. After sending people home, we checked it out."

"That's when we found the—"

Liam's head whipped toward Savage. "He's in the conference room."

"You've seen him?" I asked.

"Naw. Fucking brimstone hit our goddamned noses as soon as we walked in," said Savage.

Pandora slipped her hand into mine, and we started down the hall. Liam grabbed her elbow before we got too far. "You ain't taking her in there."

"That's not—"

"What if it's a motherfucking ambush, Axel?" Savage warned. "Death could have her out of here before we could act."

"He's right." Pandora touched my arm. "I'll wait here. Remember, I have faith in you. If you need me—if you need any of us—we'll come running." She looked over at Liam and then at Savage. "Nobody will stop us."

My gaze bounced to Hunter. He bobbed his head, echoing her sentiment. "What did I tell you? I'll be right outside the goddamned door."

"I got this," I said, still trying to reassure myself, and started down the hall again.

Liam called out, "Despite what I said, if you need us . . ."

Without stopping or turning around, I said, "I know."

Feeling like I was walking a deadly path, I forced my feet forward. The closer I got to the conference room, the warmer it grew. Sweat covered my forehead and dripped down my back. As I crossed the threshold, I peeled off my jacket, wishing I could crack open a window too.

Across from me, on the far side of the table, sat a huge figure. At first glance, I nearly mistook the man for Roman Bishop. He was just as debonair and just as mysterious as the mage. This being, however, was as tall as any hellhound but much wider. His charcoal-gray suit, dark shirt, and matching tie were immaculate and appeared to be tailored just for him. He lifted his chin, and I noticed the chiseled, broody features and eyes so dark they resembled pools of ink. A too-bright toothy grin spread over his angular, clean-shaven face.

"I'm assuming you must be the one called Monte." His voice was gravelly and deep like a death knell—appropriate, considering the circumstances.

"I am."

Death extended a large hand and pointed his finger to a chair at the end of the table. "Please, sit. We have a lot to discuss."

Part of me was defiant, wanting to hold my ground. But my grandmother's advice played in my head—*success comes with politeness.* Reluctantly, I pulled out the seat, turned it around, and straddled it.

"How did you find her?" I asked.

"Valid question. Let's just say I received a tip."

Shade.

"He is my employee, after all." Before I could say anything else, Death held up a palm. "This will go quicker if I go first." He studied me for a long, uncomfortable moment before continuing. "Are you aware that Takara broke the law?"

I was prepared for Death to play unfairly. He'd use whatever tool he could to get what he wanted. My role was to act accordingly and let him think I would capitulate. Problem was, I didn't want to be nice or act dumb. When I remembered that Pandora was counting on me, I forced the words out of my mouth. "What law would that be?"

"Shinigami aren't permitted to leave the realm unless they are on assignment," he informed me. "No one approved her departure."

I clenched and unclenched my jaw a few times, struggling to keep control. "I was under the impression that she's on a personal holiday."

Death's thin lips curled up. "Her kind do not have the luxury of such things." He paused for a beat or two, then waved his hand in the air. "But that's neither here nor there. Even if it was possible for Pandora to enjoy a vacation, I assure you, her former boss wouldn't let her."

"Former?" Since when did Pandora *not* work for Madame Death?

"Takara is no longer an employee of Izanami." He stared at me. "She belongs to *me*."

My hand balled into a fist. "Pandora is nobody's property."

Death moved his head up and down. "I see what's happened. Tell me, shifter, are you accustomed to fucking another man's bride-to-be?"

The entity was pushing the boundaries of decency. It took every ounce of strength I could summon to keep from going off—and probably getting my ass killed.

"So does that mean you properly proposed to Pandora? Did she accept your ring?"

Death barely flinched. "Touché. I could ask the same questions of you. May I call you Monte?"

"It doesn't matter to me. Not like we're about to become friends." Enemies? Most definitely.

"True, but I do like to appear approachable to those who oppose me. What is the saying so common these days?" He tilted his head to one side and ran a hand over his perfectly coiffed black hair. "Ah, politically correct? No, I don't believe that's right either. Amicable? Yes, that's the word."

"Like I said, it doesn't matter."

What mattered was getting this farce of a meeting over and done. Just being in the room with Death challenged my patience and common sense.

He thrummed his long fingers on the table for a few moments. "Trivial concerns might not be important to you, but they do mean a great deal to me. You'll find that the survivors of your beloved town will share an interest in minor issues once I decimate this haven. People will ask if I extended the fucking olive branch before I wiped Havenwood Falls off the map. I'd like them to think I did."

I scrubbed a hand over my face. It was obvious he wouldn't answer my questions. Maybe I should just say what I had to say and take it from there.

"I'd advise against that course of action," Death announced. "It's always best to consider every word that comes out of your mouth. And before you ask, I heard your thoughts. I've listened to them since your arrival by that infernal means of transportation you're so fond of. Frankly, your constant rambling is giving me a major headache."

For the sake of all that was righteous, I let that revelation slide. There were more important things to discuss.

"Don't you care about Pandora's happiness?" I asked.

Death laughed—a sound that sent an icy chill down my spine. "This isn't about her happiness. She's a damned death spirit. Happiness isn't something she's entitled to."

"What is it that you really want, Death? You could have your pick of thousands of souls crossing the veil daily. What would it take for you to strut your ass back to Hell and leave Pandora the fuck alone?"

Death folded his hands on the table and leaned forward. "I want what is mine, shifter. You could have your choice of any of the single ladies in this town. Why not choose one of them? And for the record, I don't plan on strutting my ass—as you put it—back to Hell without Takara."

The door swung wide, and Pandora stepped in. Her gaze darted from me over to Death and back again. "Are you okay, Monte?"

"I'm good."

"How sweet," Death said, slowly clapping his hands. "It's endearing that my property is concerned about a common, shit-for-brains shifter."

Pandora whirled around with her hands on her hips. "Get something straight, Death. I belong to no one!"

Death patted his jacket, removed a document, and placed it on the table. "According to this paperwork, you are mine to do with as I please. Do not consider me a heartless bastard, though. I shall give you twenty-four hours to settle your affairs before we are married."

Reaching for the parchment, I scanned the details. It spelled out, in legalese, the surrendering of Takara a.k.a. Pandora to Death. The document, surely forged in an infernal courtroom, also mentioned their upcoming nuptials. As far as I was concerned, the paperwork wasn't legal anywhere but Hell. I pushed it back to the entity.

"I don't care about your deadlines or that document," Pandora said.

Death shoved the chair back, stood, and smoothed his hand over his suit as if it were dirty. He straightened his tie and then walked toward her. "You will care soon enough. See you tomorrow, Takara."

He held out his palm. An eerie blue light sprung up and twisted into a circle. The flat shape grew wider, took on dimension, and became a swirling vortex. Death glanced over his shoulder as he stepped through the chasm. Once he cleared the threshold, it collapsed around him with an audible pop. My brothers rushed into the room.

"Are you okay?" Hunter asked as his eyes bounced around the space.

"Death returned to his realm."

Savage whipped his gaze toward me, his shoulder-length hair flying around his head. "Why?"

Pandora stared up at the hellhound. "Death is giving me twenty-four hours to settle my affairs. He'll return tomorrow to take me to Hell."

"Not happening." I looked up at Liam and Savage. "Death has some fucking-ass paperwork claiming he owns Pandora."

"Death can shove his paperwork up his ass," said Savage, pacing the floor.

Pandora gazed at all of us. "Monte, can we leave?"

Liam gave me a solemn nod, and we walked out.

Silence—and Hunter—followed us back to my house. My friend wasn't in a hurry to leave me alone. Instead, he wanted to make plans. Personally, all I wanted to do was get my hands on Shade—rearrange his bones or some shit.

Shortly after I got home, Izzie arrived with the excuse of wanting to keep Pandora company. I was grateful for the shifter. Whether it was her intention or not, she gave me a chance to speak with Hunter in private. We grabbed a six-pack from the fridge and went to the garage.

My friend twisted the cap off the longneck, took a swig, and then said, "What the fuck are you going to do, Monte?"

"Beat Death at his own game."

"Huh?"

I removed another bottle from the carton. "I plan on outsmarting Death. You've heard the expression cheating death?"

"Sure, but how?"

"We're going to let him think he's won." Unfortunately, I didn't know how to get one over on the entity.

CHAPTER 15

MONTE

Two hours and a six-pack later, we were no closer to formulating a real plan against Death. All we had was a fail-safe should things go south.

"What if we contacted Roman?" Hunter suggested.

"No," I said. "Help from him comes at a price too steep to pay."

The door to the garage creaked open, and Pandora entered. "Do you know what time it is?"

Hunter glanced at his phone. "Shit. It's after three. Izzie's gonna—"

"No, she's not," Pandora said. "She fell asleep on the sofa."

"Go home, Hunter. Take Izzie and get some sleep. We have time before Death returns. I'll talk to you later."

He nodded and quickly walked out.

"You should sleep too," Pandora said.

"I'm not tired." I held my hand out to her. When she grabbed it, I pulled her closer. "There is something you should know."

She gave me a tired smile. "What's that?"

"No matter what happens tomorrow, never forget this moment." I cupped her face and kissed her deeply, trying to pour every emotion I felt into the kiss. I'd made my decision, and Pandora was the path I wanted to be on.

Breaking away first, she gazed into my eyes and pushed the hair off my forehead. "I want to be on that path with you, but if—"

"Shh." I covered her lips with my finger. "None of that matters." I glanced down for a moment, looking for the right words. "Pandora, it's been a long time since anyone made me feel the way you do. Some would say it's too soon, while others would swear I'm rambling like a dying man, but I love you. Wherever you end up—here with me or in Hell with Death—don't forget that. I won't stop fighting until I find a way for us to be together again."

A tear slipped from her eye. "You're not rambling or dying, Montezuma Tayute. I have waited for you for over a century. We'll figure this out."

PANDORA

Monte was gone when I awakened. For a moment, I panicked and thought he'd abandoned me. After I took a deep breath, I realized that it was fear motivating my thoughts—a deep-seated fear of what was yet to come.

I made myself a cup of coffee and called Hope. Fortunately, she picked up on the first ring.

"Hi, Pandora," she said sluggishly.

"Are you okay?"

"Just tired. I've been doing double duty without you here."

"I'm sorry."

"Don't be. Madame has paid well for the extra work. How are things going with you?"

"Monte met with Death last night." I took a sip from the mug and curled up into the corner of the sofa.

"How did that go?"

"Did you know Izanami terminated my services?"

"She did?" Disbelief slipped into Hope's voice. "I didn't know that was possible."

"Well, Death had the paperwork."

"What kind of paperwork? Did you see it?"

"No. Monte did. Why?"

"Pandora, either get a look at it yourself or check with Toshi. I don't believe Madame would—or could—sign over an employee. We're not property."

I disconnected the call, and immediately contacted Toshi. After the phone rang for a solid minute, I almost hung up.

"H-hello?"

"Toshi?"

"Yes." He yawned. "Who is this?"

Shit. I must have gotten him out of bed. "It's Pandora."

He exhaled loudly and static hit my ear. "You're fortunate that I like you, Takara-chan. It's way too early for phone calls."

I set my cup on the coffee table. "Then I'll make it quick. Death claims that Madame terminated my services and gave me to him."

"I'm afraid someone's lying to you. I do all of Madame's record keeping, and I promise you that no such document exists. Besides, such an agreement implies that you're property to be bought and sold."

"Will you check for me?"

"Hold on."

I heard shuffling in the background and then the repetitive click-click of typing. "You're fortunate that I keep my laptop close." More typing and then he said, "Mm-hmm."

"What?"

"Like I said, the paperwork is false. You were created for Death. No documents were necessary."

But Death said . . .

"Takara-chan, did you see these so-called documents? Maybe it was a license for marriage."

That had to be it. Of course, Monte didn't know that. Death was using the paper for his benefit. Suddenly, I had an idea. "Toshi, I need you to tell me everything you know about the entity, including what he does for entertainment."

As soon as Monte came home, I practically pounced on him. "I might have an answer."

He hugged and kissed me before setting me on my feet. "If it includes—"

"Get your head out of the gutter." I took his hand and tugged him over to the sofa. "Death is cheating. That paperwork he showed you wasn't real."

"How do you know that?"

"I phoned Madame's assistant. Toshi handles all her business deals."

Monte grinned. "So how do we use this information?"

"Do you know how to play blackjack?"

"Does a fish swim?"

"Huh?"

"Never mind," he said, ignoring my confusion. "I've been playing since I could count. Why?"

"Death enjoys playing the game. He claims that he can't lose."

Monte scoffed. "That's because he reads his opponents' thoughts. I count cards, but that won't hold up against mind reading."

"It will if you shield your thoughts," I stated.

"I never learned—"

"But you *can* learn. You're smart, Monte." I squeezed his hand. "Call Hunter. I'm sure he'll help."

∽

MONTE

At midnight, Death met Hunter, Pandora, and me at the clubhouse. He sat in the same spot with the same shit-eating grin plastered on his swarthy face.

"Takara, I trust your affairs are in order, and we can leave soon?"

"Not so fast," I said. "I have a wager."

The entity sat taller. "Do tell."

"Blackjack. Five hands. Winner of the fifth hand takes all."

"And what do you have to offer me?"

I glanced at Pandora, and she nodded. "My life. But if I win, I get Pandora and your deal with Madame Death is null and void."

"Interesting, but let's do three hands. I don't like waiting around for my prize."

Hunter nodded as he removed a pack of cards from his jacket. I would have played one hand, but I didn't want to appear cocky.

My friend shuffled the cards while I constructed a wall around my thoughts.

Hunter glanced from Death to me. "Ready?"

Death looked across the table. He opened his mouth, and then his thick eyebrows touched. He scratched at his temple.

"Problem?" I asked.

"No, no." He rubbed a hand over his lips, scrunched his nose, and said, "Deal."

I knew what his issue was, but I couldn't dwell on it. Hunter dealt to Death first. Carefully, I watched. My opponent had an ace of spades displayed. He checked the other card and said, "Hit me."

Hunter dealt my hand—another ace. The card beneath was the jack of spades. "Hold."

My friend smiled and flipped over the dealer's cards—twenty-three. We both looked over at Death as he turned over his hand. "The win goes to the shifter."

Death grumbled. "Again."

Once more, Hunter shuffled the deck and dealt the cards. And just like the first time, Death lost.

"This is the last hand, gents. Winner takes all," Hunter said and began dealing.

"Stop!" Death flicked his wrist and a brand new pack of cards appeared on the table. "Use these."

My friend gathered the ones he'd already dealt and put them aside. He carefully studied the ones provided by Death. "These seem legit."

Counting cards didn't require a specific deck, but playing more than one hand from it was necessary. Instead of focus, I would have to rely on skill and hopefully a little luck.

Death ended up with the two of hearts as his top card. "Hit me." He checked his hand. "Again." He looked again, and a smile crossed his face. "Hold."

Death had to be bluffing. Chances were slim that he'd hit with that amount. Hunter dealt my hand—I had twenty. "Hold."

My friend shot me his lopsided grin. "What happens if dealer wins, and the two of you lose?"

I turned to Death.

"He's your friend. I'll let him call it," the entity said.

That was shocking.

Hunter flipped his hand over. Twenty-one.

Death revealed his hand. He had nineteen. Gladly, I turned over my cards.

"Technically," Hunter began, "Monte beat you. He came closest."

Pandora ran to my side. A chair scraped the floor, and Death shoved to his feet. Instead of using a portal like the last time he was there, he stormed toward the door.

Hunter clapped a hand down on my shoulder. "We did it, man."

"Yeah, we did."

It was the thought that remained in my head as we walked to the truck, but my gut told me that something—or someone—followed us.

"Not so fast, shifter."

I whirled around and saw Death standing at the edge of the parking lot. Hunter stopped on one side of me, while Pandora stood on the other.

"What do you want?" I said, sounding braver than I felt.

"I. Don't. Lose."

"Here's a news—" The sentence hung in my throat as my knees buckled.

Pandora screamed.

Then everything went black.

PANDORA

I felt Monte's spirit leaving his body. There was still time to save him. Ignoring Hunter and that asshole of an entity coming for me, I placed my hand on Monte's chest and called upon the Kami, the collective Shinto spirits.

"Please allow this man to live." My heart hurt, but we discussed the possibility. It was my last ditch effort to keep him on earth. "I trade my life for Monte Tayute's."

His eyes fluttered but didn't open. A hand landed on my shoulder, and I looked up.

"Why would you do this? He means *everything* to me," I said.

Death crouched beside me and tapped Monte's chest. "He won't die."

Confusion hit me as the entity spoke like he saved Monte. The bastard was only responsible for killing him. "I saved Monte, not—"

Ignoring me, he stood and said, "You won't die either. It's over."

As the entity walked into the shadows, Monte stirred. "Pandora? Are we—"

"No. We're alive." I glanced up at Hunter. "Help him. I'll be back."

I ran behind Death. "Wait, Death!"

He stopped but didn't look at me. "Call me Azrael."

"Azrael?"

"It's my assigned name. Death is merely my function."

"Oh." Silence filled the air for an uncomfortable minute before I said, "Thank you."

The being faced me. "Unnecessary words."

"Is this truly over, or do I need to report—"

He lifted his enormous palm. "You don't belong to me, and you no longer serve Izanami."

"I don't understand. I traded my life for Monte's."

"No. The Kami reached out, but I stopped them."

"But why?"

"Because I felt your heart and your pain. You love that shifter. If I took you away from him, you'd be miserable."

True.

"Besides, you were never meant for this line of work. I don't know how it is that Izanami created you. Takara, you have a heart and a soul. You belong in *this* world."

Death's—Azrael's—words should have made me happy, but they didn't. A nervous twitch flared in my stomach. "What will happen to me?"

"Live a long life, Takara. As long as you stay in this town, nothing bad will ever happen to you."

"And Monte?"

"The shifter's heart now beats for the both of you. When he draws his last breath, so will you. Both of you will remain together throughout eternity."

Gravel crunched behind me. His familiar hands wrapped around my waist. "How do we thank you?"

Azrael tilted his head to the side. "Be good to each other. Stay faithful. But, shifter, if you ever hurt her . . . If you ever make Takara unhappy, I will sever this arrangement, and your soul will be mine."

"Understood," Monte said.

"Azrael, why would you grant us a long life?" I asked.

"Because I love you enough to let you go." When I remained speechless, he continued, "I have loved you since the first day of your creation. I knew you were special, and I waited patiently for you to be mine. But forcing you to return to Hell would not make you love me."

It was the last thing Azrael said before he opened up another portal and disappeared.

Monte leaned down and said into my ear, "Thank you."

"For what?"

"Loving me."

"How could I not?" I intertwined my fingers with his. "I'm kind of stuck with you."

"But it's the best kind of stuck there could ever be."

We hope you enjoyed this story in the Havenwood Falls world featuring a variety of supernatural creatures. Havenwood Falls is a collaborative effort by multiple authors. If you haven't already, be sure to read *Taming the Beast* by Nadirah Foxx (continue on for an excerpt).

You may also enjoy these other books in the Havenwood Falls Sin & Silk series:

Plans Laid Bare by J.D. Nelson
Damned Allure by Justine Winter
Savage Salvation by Kristie Cook
Chase the Flames by Desiree Lafawn

Also try the signature line, Havenwood Falls, the historical paranormal line, Legends of Havenwood Falls, and the local supernatural college, Sun & Moon Academy.

Stay up to date at www.HavenwoodFalls.com

ABOUT THE AUTHOR

Nadirah Foxx is the alter ego for author SF Benson. This persona is fond of dark, twisted romance featuring suspense and adventure. She also loves a good paranormal tale. Her characters are always flawed, but they always find a way around the obstacles and demons of life.

Connect with Nadirah on:
Facebook: https://www.facebook.com/NadirahFoxx/
Twitter: @nadirahfoxx
Blog: https://nadirahfoxx.wordpress.com/blog

ACKNOWLEDGMENTS

Thank you so much for reading Pandora and Monte's story. I love including mythology in my paranormal tales. For this one, I used Japanese folklore. It was fun adding a new twist to shinigami lore.

A special thank you goes out to all of the Havenwood Falls authors who allowed me to feature their characters. As always, I appreciate the help!

I thank my publisher, Kristie Cook, and editor, Liz Ferry. They continue to impart valuable lessons.

Thanks go to my cover artist, Regina Wamba/Mae I Design. She captured my idea perfectly.

I thank my husband and daughter for putting up with me through the process.

Last but not least, I thank my parents—for without them, none of this is possible.

AN EXCERPT

Taming the Beast (A Havenwood Falls Sin & Silk Novella) by Nadirah Foxx

Stealing from a mafia boss is the dumbest thing Izzie Itzae has ever done. Getting lost in the mountains is a close second. But both events pale compared to meeting the one male she's not ready for. As a nagual shifter waiting for her first transformation, Izzie's anger and frustration grow every day—bonding with her soul mate is the last thing she needs.

Hunter James knows bonding is exactly what Izzie needs, and he's more than ready for her. He's dreamed of her often, while his shaman grandfather's had visions of the female who can break the family curse. Hunter doesn't care that Izzie's a late bloomer—in fact, he's eager for the challenge. As long as Izzie can handle his brand of proclivities, he's sure he can tame her inner beast.

When they meet, the chemistry is instantaneous, no matter how much Izzie tries to deny it. But obstacles abound, including Hunter's ex-girlfriend, who will do anything to get Hunter back in her bed, including stooping to dark magic.

A threat to Izzie's life is the ultimate test for her. To save herself and Hunter, she must choose—cling to her stubbornness or give in to her heart's truth. But only one will tame her beast.

TAMING THE BEAST

BY NADIRAH FOXX

It's just my luck to end up in the middle of nowhere without a damn cell signal. For the last hour, I've been trying to make heads or tails of a map—how primitive. Leaning my palms against the SUV hood, I push my dark hair out of my face and think about how this was supposed to be an uncomplicated trip allowing me to check out the fall colors and escape.

The plan seemed simple enough. Catch a flight out of New York, rent a car (now with an empty gas tank, although it was full an hour ago), and hide away in my best friend Senora's cabin. In all fairness, she warned me the roads could be tricky, but I didn't listen. Thought I could rely on my phone's GPS. Staring down at the device, I realize my stupidity. I forgot mountains and signal strength don't mix.

I'm ready to pitch the damned thing when a distant rumbling grabs my attention. A huge pickup truck comes into sight. The shiny black vehicle stops inches from me, and a female jumps out of the cab. The tall redhead, dressed in jeans and a tank top, comes around the front of the truck.

"Everything okay?" she asks with a wide smile. Her sparkling gray-blue eyes appear friendly, but my guard, as always, is up.

"I'm good," I blurt, not wanting her to get too close for both our sakes. "Just need to figure out where I'm going."

"Really?" The stranger points to the car. "You're out of gas and lost."

"How the—" My words freeze when I notice the pendant around her neck—a green jade coyote. The familiar nagual pulse passes through me, and the tension rolls off my shoulders. She's a kindred spirit. Most likely she took one look at the map and figured out my problem.

"I'm sure you can take care of yourself, but it'll be dark soon," she offers. "Nights can be freezing, not to mention the other beasts roaming these parts."

Confrontations aren't ideal for me. At least until my transformation happens. Then I'll be able to go up against other creatures—even other naguals if needed. "I suppose I could use a ride."

"Where you headed?"

"Grand Junction."

The female laughs. "Sorry. You *are* lost. That's north of here and about two hours away. How about this? I'll take you to town, where you can stay overnight. In the morning, I'll point you in the right direction."

It's tempting to say no, but fate speeds up time, sending the sun into a quick descent. The choice is made for me. I open the back door, drag out my suitcase, and roll it over to the truck.

The redhead hops in and cranks the ignition. Over the interior noise, she introduces herself. "My name's Cheresse."

"Izzie."

"What brings you to Colorado?"

"Just a getaway." It's all I'm offering. Being on the run makes trust precarious.

"I get it." Cheresse gives me a sideways glance. "We all have secrets, but if you want to share . . . Just saying." She slips into silence.

After a few miles, Cheresse leaves the state highway and turns onto a two-lane county road lined on both sides by forest. The welcome sign for Havenwood Falls comes into sight. As the truck passes the layered stone and black metal lettering marker, my pendant —a jade quetzal—heats. The sensation startles me. Automatically, I touch my neck. Common sense would have been to tuck the totem beneath my shirt—avoiding the possibility of any knowledgeable nagual discovering I'm powerless—but I don't always act with sagacity. I'm a would've-should've-could've type of female. Unfortunately, the gesture draws Cheresse's attention.

"Don't worry. That's normal. My totem heats up every time I enter town, too. It's just the magic here."

"Magic?" Whoa. A town with magic? So the tales I heard growing up were true. Although I grew up with shapeshifters and shamans, I had no experience with the mystical arts. I thought the stories of a magical town were as wacky as the "tobacco" the elders smoked.

"Havenwood Falls is a safe place for supernaturals. You'll need a visitor's tattoo to remain in town."

"Why? I don't do ink. Nothing against those who do. It's just not my thing."

"Whether it's your thing or not isn't the point. The tattoos let the leaders know who's in town. For some of us, there's an extra benefit to having one."

Somehow I seriously doubt if some ink is going to help my situation, but I'll play along. "Like?"

"Take the vampires, for instance. It allows them to go out in the sun." Cheresse looks over at me. "Before you ask, it won't help you."

My defenses immediately go up. This female nagual can't possibly know anything about me.

"I can't read your thoughts, but I sense your immaturity. If you don't mind my saying, you seem a little old not to have transformed yet. You're what, twenty-two? Twenty-three?" Cheresse's tone isn't condescending, just annoying.

"Almost twenty-five," I mutter, strumming my fuchsia-colored nails against the door.

Transformation usually happens for nagual females at twenty-one. So, yeah, I'm a little late. Before my grandmother died, she told me it wasn't unusual to mature later in life. I'm not worried. Just pissed. All the damned time. It's an unfortunate trait of an immature nagual— intense anger as my beast struggles to emerge. Mine has been trying for three years. Anger doesn't adequately describe my fury.

Nothing eradicates the intense negative feelings crawling beneath my skin. Mom also warned me, before she died, that there would be days like this. The closer the age of metamorphosis gets—puberty for naguals—the more erratic my emotions. Maybe my birthday, in a week, will end this constant roller coaster of emotions.

I bite my tongue and hang on to the comments I'd like to throw at Cheresse.

Sadly, she doesn't know how to keep her mouth shut. "Hey, I'm sorry. Some of us are late bloomers. I had mine three years ago."

Good for you.

Chatty females like Cheresse is why I'm best friends with an empusa. The creature of the night is more likely to chat up a male victim than spend time conversing with me. Senora and I tolerate each other, giving space when it's needed. My eyes slide toward the clock on the truck dashboard—nine o'clock. *Mental note: call Senora when I get settled.*

The darkening landscape changes as we crest the ridge up ahead. Inky black mountains—replacing the riot of oranges, reds, and browns—surround the town like an ominous silhouette. Cheresse drives past a housing development decorated with eerie orange lights and ornaments. Lots of jack-o'-lanterns, cut-out ghosts, spider webs, and even a few animatronic figures adorn the yards. In my haste to leave New York, I nearly forgot about Halloween.

Cheresse takes the right fork in the road, and I get a glimpse of what the small town has to offer—a townhouse-and-villa complex, a three-story high school, a shopping center, and an apartment complex. Every structure, including the closed shops in the town square, is decked out for the holiest of holidays for supes.

The car comes to a stop in front of a large Victorian manor with its own creepy, very realistic looking cemetery in the yard. Cheresse laughs. "It's just decoration. In Havenwood Falls, we take the holiday seriously."

Instead of her words imparting comfort, they piss me off further. I don't appreciate anyone finding humor in my discomfort. My fists clench, and I give a low growl.

Cheresse pays no attention to my anger—supes rarely do. Once another supernatural discovers that I'm an immature nagual, they disregard my fury, treating me like a petulant child.

"This is Whisper Falls Inn," she points out. "You should be able to get a room for the night. Michaela Petran is the owner. She's okay, if you don't mind vamps."

"I don't." Hey, my friend is a lot worse than a vampire.

Cheresse opens the door and freezes. "Shit."

"Problem?"

"My ex . . . my *boy*friend is here. That's his bike."

"Oh," I say, exiting the cab.

Headed in our direction is a handsome, slightly muscular male with wavy black hair and penetrating turquoise eyes. The sexy scent of sandalwood tickles my nose. Our eyes meet, and his lips curl up. Then he notices Cheresse, and a frown crosses his face.

She plasters on an obviously fake smile and says, "Hi, Hunter."

He keeps a considerable distance from the ginger-haired female. Odd if they're supposed to be a couple. In a low voice, he says, "Cheresse."

The palpable tension between them is thick, but it's none of my business. Instead, I grab my suitcase and try to ignore the warmth rising out of my totem. As I get closer to him, however, a sudden flash catches my eye. Hunter's pendant—a jade puma—glows. Cheresse's totem remains solid while mine scorches my skin.

Not good.

There's only one reason for totems to react like this.

My gut tells me to run for the hills, but I'm here now, and Hunter's blocking the path to the inn. Cheresse slips past me and grabs his hand, but he doesn't try to hold hers. His focus is on me.

"I don't think we've met," he says to me.

"No. We haven't." I leave it at that. The name stitched on his jacket—Trapper—is ironic. Getting tangled up with him would indeed have me trapped.

Might be nice.

"Silly me," Cheresse chimes in. "*Isis*, this is my boyfriend Hunter. Hunter, this is my friend Isis."

If we're friends, the bimbo would know my name. "Actually, it's Izzie."

"I'm just dropping her off," Cheresse continues. "And then I'll head home and make dinner for us."

Hunter shakes his head. "Cheresse, that's not happening. You know we're not . . ."

Things just got interesting. I let my hand slip off the luggage handle.

Cheresse's voice trembles a bit. "Never mind him. We had a nasty fight, but that's over." Cheresse slips her hands around Hunter's arm and tries to pull him closer, but he doesn't budge. "Let me make it up to you, sweetheart."

Hunter gives me a *don't believe it* stare.

The clueless female persists. "Okay. We'll meet up later. I'll prepare something for Izzie and me instead. Give us a chance to get caught up."

Marijuana may be legal here, but I think this female is smoking something a lot more potent. We have nothing to catch up on.

"That's enough, Cheresse." Hunter steps away from her before touching my forearm. "It was nice to meet you, Izzie. Don't be a stranger."

He saunters toward his bike, and I notice his jacket insignia—the words "Swords of the Infernal Night" with a picture of a sword sticking through a skull. A biker. Why did I have to attract *his* attention? Motorcycle clubs are notorious for treating women poorly. The males are players, and I don't have time for those games.

"Hunter!" Cheresse calls behind him. "Don't forget our agreement."

Hunter whirls around. His hooded gaze bounces from Cheresse to me and back again. "Consider it void."

He straddles his bike, cranks it up, and drives off.

I start to ask what he meant, but think better of it. "Thanks for the lift."

Cheresse loses her polite demeanor. Looking down her nose, she says, "Don't even think about it. He's mine."

Cutting my dark eyes at the statuesque female, I'm ready to deliver my own warning. *Unnecessary.* My plans don't include the shit unfolding between the couple. Emotions, however, churn like a storm brewing beneath my skin. I don't possess powers, but I still want to beat the crap out of Cheresse. Instead of ripping into the stupid female, I roll my suitcase toward the building.

The inn's interior is an enchanting marriage of the past and the present. I'm appreciative of the modern fixtures and the centuries old architecture. Behind the desk is an attractive female with brown hair and odd gray-green eyes. Moroi. Vampire.

"Can I help you?" she says.

"You must be Michaela. I was told I could get a room."

"Great." She reaches for a large book. "How long are you staying?"

Before I can speak, my phone buzzes with a message.

"Excuse me." I remove the device from my back pocket and peer at the screen.

Senora Graves: Izzie, you need to stay away. Chekhov was here looking for you. He said if he ever sees you again, you're dead.

I'm tempted to send Senora a reply, but I can't. Kazimir Chekhov undoubtedly has his goons out, tracking my whereabouts. The man has three million reasons to find me. Senora is powerful, but I won't knowingly compromise her.

Tomorrow, I'll purchase a burner phone. For now, I need to find a more permanent place to stay. Facing the owner, I ask, "Any possibility you have something for long-term stays?"

A cautious gaze rakes over me for a moment before she says, "I have a one-bedroom cottage available. We just need to get you signed in with the Registry."

"Registry?"

Michaela leans over the counter and lowers her voice. "The Court likes to know where the supes are in town."

"How did you know?"

She points to my neck. "I'll call Addie to come do your tattoo."

Minutes later, I'm pacing the floor instead of unpacking, unable to focus on the task. I still can't wrap my mind around the whole course of events—getting my ass lost and then hopping into a truck with a stranger. *Fuck! I left the rental car! How the hell am I going to get that back?* No way am I spending my recent fortune on somebody's used vehicle.

A knock on the cottage door disrupts my mental scolding. On the other side is a girl around my age dressed in ripped jeans, a thick black sweater, and knee-high boots. Her light brown hair is in a ponytail, and her brown eyes blink at me from behind a pair of black-framed glasses. She's carrying an old leather satchel.

Shit. Guarantee she's the chick wanting to do the damned tattoo.

What kind of town requires ink to live in it? Another reason for me to hit the road as soon as the sun comes up.

"Izzie?" she asks.

"Maybe." Contempt curls in my voice.

The girl's gaze narrows briefly. "My name is Addie, and I'm here to do your tattoo. Maybe we could talk first? I'll answer the questions you have."

Tilting my head to the side, I ask, "How did you know?"

"Part of my job is answering questions for all newcomers. I assumed you'd have some." She looks over my shoulder. "Can I come in?"

I take a deep breath. This girl isn't responsible for my misfortune. Stepping to one side, I say, "Sure."

Addie enters the living room, takes a seat on the sofa, and places her bag on the floor. "I realize all of this is overwhelming. Ask me anything. I'll do my best to fill you in."

Although I should feel relieved not to be doing the ink right away, I'm not. The events of the day have me so worked up. Usually when I get this bad, I find someone to fuck me hard—get me off. What do I do here?

"I can help you," Addie says quietly.

"Sorry, I'm not into females."

The girl smiles. "I'm not offering what you think. Sit down and close your eyes."

As soon as I take a seat beside her, I feel Addie's hand on my arm followed by a tingling. It mixes with the brewing storm beneath my skin. A sense of calm dissipates the fury. I open my eyes.

"What did you do?"

"It's a lot easier for us to talk without your anger. Your emotions surround you like a cloud." The pleasantness suddenly drops from her voice. "I'm here to help you, but don't mistake my kindness."

"Got it." Last thing I need is to get on the wrong side of a *bruja*.

Addie continues, "My family, the Beaumonts, is one of the founding families of the Luna Coven. That's the main coven of witches in town."

I sit back. "Witches, vampires, nagual . . . What else lives here?"

"Shifters, mages, fae, sirens, gargoyles . . . pretty much any species and subspecies you can think of."

Interesting. Back in New York, I never knew what was lurking around me until it was usually too late. Once, I made the mistake of pissing off a *bruja*. She threatened to send me back in time to the Maya. Thankfully, Senora saved me from spending the rest of eternity with the ancestors.

"So, only supernaturals live here?"

"No. The population here is split, with half being humans. For some reason, the town tends to attract nonhumans. We do our best to keep the town secret, but it hasn't stopped supes from finding us. According to legend, it's always been that way."

Sorry, I'm not convinced. Supernaturals stay hidden for a reason. There's no way that we can coexist openly with humans. Shit happens. "Next you'll tell me that everyone here gets along."

"That's what's *supposed* to happen." Addie doesn't say anything else, and I wonder what she's hiding.

"Tell me why getting this tattoo is so important?"

Addie reaches into her bag and pulls out a tattoo kit. "All supernaturals are marked when they come to Havenwood Falls. The design signs you into the Registry so the Court knows who's in town. Visitors get a temporary tattoo."

"Court?"

"The Court of the Sun and the Moon. They try to make sure we all get along." She places the kit on the coffee table.

"And when that doesn't happen?"

"It's not something you need to worry about." Addie's gaze darts away from me. "We have our rules, mostly don't kill the humans." She looks in my direction again. "Besides that, think of Havenwood Falls as a safe place. You'll find more naguals here. They'll be able to help you through your transformation."

"You can tell?"

Addie gives me a pointed look. "Have you been listening?"

"Witch. Right." How could I forget?

Removing a sketch pad, Addie says, "Let's talk about your design. From the look of your totem, I suspect you might want something permanent. I can make it invisible if you prefer."

Her words alert me. "What about my totem?"

Addie sighs deeply and gives me a thoughtful expression. "Your soul mate is here. Because of my job, I've had to learn about all the different supernaturals and magic. From what I remember about nagual tradition, when you discover the one meant for you, your totem glows."

And there it is. The main reason I need to leave this town—the sooner, the better.

"Any idea of what design you want?"

An invisible design sounds better than having ink splattered over my skin. I'm not totally convinced that this is in my best interest, but I ask, "Can you do anything Mayan?"

"What are you thinking?"

"Something with Ixchel, the moon goddess."

Addie laughs.

"What's so funny?"

"You just told me who your mate is."

My eyes narrow. "How?"

"Your choice in tattoo. Kinich Ahau is Hunter James's design."

Damn. That's the sun god Ixchel's husband. I am so screwed.

Purchase *Taming the Beast* where books are sold.

www.ingramcontent.com/pod-product-compliance
Lightning Source LLC
Chambersburg PA
CBHW052004170626
46808CB00007B/2777